RIFKA
GROWS UP

RIFKA
GROWS UP

Written and illustrated by
CHAYA M. BURSTEIN

BONIM BOOKS
New York ● London

Library of Congress Cataloging in Publication Data

Burstein, Chaya M
  Rifka grows up.

  Sequel to Rifka bangs the teakettle.
  SUMMARY: The social upheaval prior to the Russian
Revolution touches Rifka, a twelve-year-old Jewish girl,
as she struggles to further her education.
  [1. Russia—Fiction. 2. Jews in Russia—Fiction]
PZ7.B94553Rk   [Fic]   76-41412
ISBN 0-88482-906-5

BONIM BOOKS
a division of Hebrew Publishing Company
79 Delancey Street
New York, N.Y. 10002

PRINTED IN THE UNITED STATES OF AMERICA

CONTENTS

RIFKA
GROWS UP

ONE

Rifka Skates Into Trouble

The door squeaked open and Moozeleh the goat scrambled to her feet.

A soapy cloud rolled out against the tight December air. Mama was doing the laundry.

"Tie your kerchief tighter."

"Yes, Mama — now can I go?"

At the sound of Rifka's voice, Moozeleh shook the snow out of her white coat and braced her skinny legs, ready to play.

"And pull up your stockings, you'll catch cold."

"All right, Mama. Raizelleh's waiting — can I go?"

"And don't stay long. You have to study for your lesson with Shayndel tomorrow."

"Mama, I know — can I..."

"Go, go...but be careful, don't fall."

The door slammed shut on Mama's final words and Rifka took a flying leap from the porch to land "thlomp!" almost on top of the goat.

But bundled as she was, Rifka could have landed on a herd of goats without being dented. Bright, blue eyes and a wide, freckle-splattered nose showed beneath her wool kerchief, but the rest of the wiry ("skinny," said her mother) twelve-year-old girl was buried under sweaters, jacket, three skirts and petticoats, long woolen bloomers and stockings. Each year when

1

the bitter, Russian winter settled onto the small town of Savran, the townspeople suddenly grew fat, wrapped in layers of most of the clothing they owned.

"Meh-eh," Moozeleh murmured as Rifka skipped past, her braids and kerchief flying.

"Not now, I'm busy," she sang out.

The wooden gate creaked open and swung shut, almost catching Moozeleh's tail as she galloped after Rifka.

"Meh-eh-eh-eh!" she protested. Her small, black hooves clip-clopped on the packed snow close behind Rifka's boots.

"I can't play, Moozeleh. I'm going ice skating. See?" Rifka swung the new wooden skates that her big brother Velvl had sent her right under the goat's curious nose.

Aha! A tug of war. Moozeleh's eyes sparkled and she chomped her strong, yellow teeth onto the smooth wood and dug her hooves in for a big pull.

"Ay, ay, ay—no, no...let go!" Rifka pulled back, slipping and sliding on the snow while she searched through her layers of clothes. She hauled an emergency crust of bread from a deep apron pocket and tossed it back past the goat, who quickly dropped the skate to chase the food.

In a flurry of snow Rifka turned and galloped on, past Aunt Miriam's tiny, gray house, past Reb Leib's fancy two story house and through the marketplace, dodging around herring barrels and pushcarts.

"Like a wild goat," Hannah the vegetable seller scolded after her. "A twelve-year-old girl, practically a bride, and she runs like a wild goat!"

"I have new skates," Rifka shouted over her shoulder as she thudded down the last street before the Savrankeh River.

Most of the year this modest stream wandered in a muddy,

half circle around the town of Savran. Housewives met on its sandy bank to gossip and scrub laundry, Lazer the water carrier filled his barrel here when the well was crowded, and storks built nests in its reeds. It had a job to do and it knew its place, just like everything and everyone in the community. Only in early spring the Savrankeh got drunk, swollen and proud with melting snow, rising up into the town, filling the marketplace and flooding the houses.

Today the river was a gleaming sheet of ice, jumping with people. There were farm boys from beyond the river, stealing away from chores, town boys like Rifka's younger brother Elli, playing hooky from school, girls who should have been at home, kneading bread dough or babysitting or flicking feathers from a chicken. Everybody was skating in a happy, bumping, shoving crowd. Their shouts echoed against the great, solemn trees on the far shore.

Where was Raizelleh? Her best friend had promised to teach her how to skate. Rifka squinted against the low winter sun, then she gave up impatiently. I don't need her, she decided — if everybody can do it, then it can't be that hard.

She carefully fastened the skates to her boots with the leather straps, just as her father had shown her. She wobbled to the edge of the ice and stepped boldly into the traffic. That is — one leg stepped boldly. The other leg shot off to the side, while the top of her sped wildly backward, arms whirling like windmill blades, and she landed with a great thump — flat on the ice.

"Clumseeeee — you'll crack the ice," a familiar voice teased. Her younger brother Elli scraped by, spraying her with slush, and was gone.

"Thanks a lot," Rifka muttered and carefully pulled herself

up, her cheeks flaming and ankles wobbling.

One, two, three, four...she counted her shaky steps in little puffs of breath as everybody else seemed to swirl and whirl past her. On five, Leibel, the baker's red-haired son, cut behind her and yanked her braid.

Thump! Rifka was down again. "Red Leb, the carrot head!" she yelled at him, to save her self-respect. Papa hadn't said it would be this hard; he thought she would be able to skate as well as the Czar himself. If the Czar went skating, he'd have twenty servants running behind him with satin pillows, and every time he wobbled, they'd push the pillows under his royal backside.

She lay and rested; there just didn't seem to be any point in getting up again. The world looked different from flat on her back. What a pretty blue the sky was, with the spikes of evergreens framing it in a zig-zagging circle. She rubbed the tender spot through three layers of skirt, petticoats and woolen bloomers. Suddenly Elli's grinning face pushed into her circle of sky.

"Is that a new way to skate? Flat on your back?"

"Be quiet and wipe your nose," she snapped. "Where's Raizelleh?"

"Over by the bridge. She wants you to come."

"Tell her to come here."

"She won't. She said you have to go there — right away!" Elli vanished in a shower of snow which settled gently on her face.

Rifka moved carefully onto her hands and knees. That felt safe. If only she could skate that way. Moozeleh was lucky to be four-legged all the time, she thought. Shakily, she hoisted herself upright. Taking tiny steps like a brittle grandmother, she moved slowly toward the uncrowded area near the bridge where summer reeds stood imprisoned in the ice.

Five...six...seven...She dared to sneak a look ahead. The gray bridge across the Savrankeh seemed to be miles away.

Thirty one...thirty two...miracle of miracles, she was still up and even daring to slide her feet a little bit.

The hubbub of voices was far behind her as she approached the bridge. Raizelleh, eyes popping with excitement and one finger at her lips, reached out for Rifka.

"Slowpoke, it took you forever. You'll miss them," she hissed, dragging her friend into the reeds.

"Did you see me?" Rifka bubbled. "I can skate!"

"Ssssh," Raizelleh clapped her hand over Rifka's mouth and nodded toward the shadows under the bridge.

Still glowing with her new accomplishment, Rifka blinked away the sunlight and squinted into the darkness. At first, she heard only the far-off shrilling of the skaters. Then a gentler, closer murmur of voices drifted in. And finally two figures sifted themselves out of the shadows, standing close together.

"It's your teacher, Shayndel," Raizelleh giggled, "with a man, a strange man."

Shayndel's flowered kerchief was pulled over her forehead and her coat collar almost hid her face, but Rifka recognized the round curve of her cheek and the eager tilt forward as she spoke.

"She's got a boyfriend, that shameless girl," Raizelleh smirked. "Wait till I tell Mama!"

Rifka jabbed her angrily.

The young man was tall and thin, with broad shoulders that stretched his coarse, peasant jacket. A fur hat partly covered his straight, blonde hair.

She had never seen him before. He was a stranger to Sav-

ran. Rifka's heart sank. Though she was only twelve, she knew that it was wrong for a girl to meet a young man secretly, without a third person around. And if the man was a stranger it could only be worse.

With heads bent toward each other they seemed to be reading from a piece of paper. Then the two figures drew even closer together and became a single shadow.

"Oooooh—they're kissing!" Raizelleh bounced up and down delightedly, her blond curls bobbing below her scarf.

"Don't be an idiot!" Rifka whispered desperately. "Let's go." She tugged at Raizelleh, but her friend pulled back.

"Kissing a stranger, maybe even a peasant," she crowed softly. "Mama always said there was something funny about Shayndel...too much education."

The young man drew away slowly. He lifted a large, gray package from the ice beside him and gave it to Shayndel. Then he turned quickly and walked out into the sunlight beyond the bridge, climbed the snow-covered bank of the river and disappeared from sight.

Shayndel had turned to watch him and the girls saw only her back, shoulders drooping, as she stood holding the box in the cold shadows.

Suddenly, Zev, the son of Chayim the cloth merchant, swooped across the ice on his makeshift wire skates, chased by Elli. They both slammed into the bridge wall. Shayndel jumped at the noise, pushed her collar even higher without turning and, clutching the package, hurried up the bank toward town.

"Hey, Zev," Raizelleh called, "I know something you don't know!"

But they were already up and scrambling away, smashing snowballs at each other.

"Hush!" Rifka pounced on her friend and yanked at a handful of curls. "Gossip is the worst sin in the whole world! Do you want God to punish you?"

Raizelleh's round eyes opened wider and her lips trembled. She could ice skate better than Rifka and she could embroider more neatly. By Savran's standards, which favored plump, pink girls and thin, studious boys, her dimpled face was prettier than Rifka's. But when it came to religion and booklearning, she had great respect for her friend.

Rifka was the only girl in their tiny town who had learned to read and write both Hebrew and Russian. She was studying the Bible and geography and history—just like any boy.

"Is gossip really such a terrible sin?" she quavered.

"Awful—worse than murder."

"But Hannah the vegetable lady gossips all day long."

"You can't even imagine what punishments the devil is preparing for such a one."

Raizelleh shuddered. "But they *were* kissing," she said finally.

"Don't be a silly goose. They were just talking with their mouths close together," Rifka insisted. "Come on, Raizelleh, you promised to teach me how to skate, and soon I'll have to go home and help Mama with the laundry."

They held hands and pushed off across the river. Rifka's ankles kept turning sideways and backwards as they moved faster and faster. Other skaters zigzagged around them until they slammed into Zev and all three fell in a tangled pile. But even then, as she laughed and struggled to get up, her head was busy worrying. Who was the stranger? What was in the package? How could her wonderful, smart, educated Shayndel meet alone with a strange man?

Later, Raizelleh and Rifka walked silently back through

town, swinging their skates. The sky was a deeper gray-blue. Puffs of smoke rose from the chimneys and supper smells burst through quickly opened and closed doors. Men and boys hurried past them on the way to the synagogue for evening prayers.

Raizelleh spoke up. "Even if they weren't kissing, she's a strange one. Mama said any girl who isn't even engaged by the age of nineteen is a strange one."

Rifka felt her face getting hot. "Your mother doesn't know anything. She thinks all a girl should do is embroider pillowcases and milk goats and get fat, waiting for a matchmaker to pick a husband for her. Shayndel is better than that. She's better than anyone in this town. She's going to work and earn enough money and then she's going to go away to the university and learn to be a doctor or a lawyer... or, or something else important."

"Ha — a lady doctor," Raizelleh snorted, "who ever heard of a lady doctor? Mama says learning should be left to boys, it'll only spoil a girl. And she says your mother is asking for trouble by letting Shayndel teach you...."

Rifka stuck her fingers in her ears, but Raizelleh's little round mouth kept talking, talking, talking.

"You're just ignorant!" Rifka yelled, snatched up her skates and ran.

At the marketplace in the center of town, Fishkeh the fish man was already rolling his barrels of herring into his wagon. Hannah the vegetable seller blew on her stiff fingers and packed potatoes into a sack.

"You, Rifkalleh," she called, "Better watch that thieving goat of yours. She nearly stole a carrot from my basket. Just once more...."

Rifka hurried past, hardly hearing.

Moozeleh, the thieving goat, climbed out from under the herring wagon, shook herself, and greeted Rifka with an affectionate "meh-meh-eh." Rifka buried her cold hands in the rough, warm fur. She began to feel better. Moozeleh butted her skirt gently and they started for home. Near Aunt Miriam's house, two hens and Kvetcher the rooster fluttered down from the fence to join them in a "home-for-supper" parade.

"It'll be all right if only Raizelleh doesn't tell her mother," Rifka thought to herself. Then she blushed guiltily as she though, "Maybe, for now, I won't tell Mama either. Why should I worry her?"

There was a tug at her arm. Moozeleh was delicately nibbling her ice skates again.

"Ignorant!" she shrieked. Raising the skates up high above her head, she ran through the yard and onto the porch.

"Mama!" she yelled, "I think I learned to skate!"

TWO

Geese for Books

"The Atlantic Ocean borders on Western Europe. The countries of Western Europe are France, Germany, Holland, England..." Rifka was counting on her fingers while she ate breakfast.

"Why do you want to know all that junk?" Elli scoffed. "My teacher, Reb Mendl, says all we have to know is enough Russian to deal with the tax collector and Fedka the policeman. He said to save the rest of our brains for the Bible and the Prayer Book."

He took another mouthful of bread and cheese. "Yesterday Reb Mendl caught red-haired Leibel reading a forbidden book. He had hidden it inside his Bible. Wow! What a thrashing he got—with the strap, not just the ruler. Right in front of everybody. And he's fourteen already, taller than Reb Mendl."

"It serves him right! Leibel made me fall on the ice yesterday," gloated Rifka. "But Elli, geography is very important. Shayndel says I have to know it to take the test for a high school certificate. And then, if I do really well, maybe someday I'll go to the university."

"Hush with your big plans, Rifkalleh," Mama interrupted, "right now, we don't even have money to buy the books you need to study from. Your Papa earns a hard living."

11

"University—phooey!" said Elli. "What I want is to be rich like Reb Leib in his two-story house with his tall silk hat and big fur coat."

"Hurry up, Elli, you'll be late for school." Mama turned away to pack his lunch in a kerchief.

Elli quickly reached for an extra lump of sugar, but it seemed that Mama had a thousand eyes, as she often reminded them, and she whacked Elli's wrist.

He settled back sadly with his single lump, grumbling, "A person can't even taste one measly lump of sugar."

He perked up a minute later. "Hey, Rifkalleh, I bet I know how Reb Leib sugars his tea."

"Mmmmmmm," said Rifka.

"He pokes his little finger in the sugar bowl to make a little hole and then he pours his tea into the hole and drinks right from the sugar bowl!"

"Yech," Rifka wrinkled her nose and went back to memorizing. "The countries of Western Europe are France, Germany, Holland....."

A piercing "waaah" from the front porch interrupted her again, followed by shrill scolding and then a loud knock at the door. Before Mama could reach the door, it swung open.

Aunt Miriam filled the entrance, her kerchief sliding over one eye, carrying the baby on her hip and firmly grabbing the wrist of her howling two-year-old, Berelleh. Loud honking sounds from the street almost drowned him out.

"Chaykeh, you must help me. I'm at my wit's end!" Miriam cried. "Please watch the children, I'm going to take the geese to the marketplace and sell them."

The wind blasted in, carrying more hoarse honking from outside.

Mama rushed to shut the door and then echoed, "Sell the geese? But Ephraim just bought them for you to fatten up over the winter. Why should you sell them now?"

"My clever husband Ephraim has too many good ideas. It's not enough that he blesses me with a baby boy each year—no evil eye should harm them," she added hastily, "Now he has to bring in geese. I can't even turn around in my kitchen before one of them pokes his head out of the coop and nips me."

Elli turned red, shaking with silent laughter and splattering a mouthful of food into his tea. "If she didn't stick out so far, they wouldn't nip!" he gasped.

Rifka smothered a giggle.

"Elli," Mama said sharply, "time for school."

"And this morning while I was getting breakfast Berelleh

was feeding his brother potato peels from the goose's dish,"
Aunt Miriam continued.

"Honk, honk, honk" clamored the geese.

"Waaa," wailed Berelleh, dancing from leg to leg, "I
wanna feed Meyer like Mama does."

"That's enough geese for me," Aunt Miriam swept on,
"even if I don't earn a groschen, even if I have to give them
away, even if I have to pay someone to take them…"

Money! Rifka gulped her hot tea and burst out, "Oh, Aunt
Miriam, could you give them to me?"

"…even if…" Aunt Miriam's voice, which was rising to
operatic heights, suddenly stopped.

"What?" she asked.

Berelleh stopped crying.

"I'd feed them and clean their coop and keep them warm.
And when they got fat enough I'd sell them and earn money
to buy my school books."

"We have no room. Where would you put them?" Mama
asked.

"I'd make room in the shed, Mama. They would keep
Moozeleh and the chickens company, and with everybody in
there the shed would stay warmer so the potatoes wouldn't
freeze."

"And I'll help you," Elli announced generously, on his
way out the door, "because I need money, too."

"No thanks, go to school," said Rifka.

"And pull your hat over your ears," Mama ordered as Elli
stamped out.

She poured a cup of tea for Aunt Miriam and smeared
black bread with cheese for Berelleh and Meyer and thought.
Rifka's great hunger for learning worried her. How would her

eager, questioning daughter settle down to her proper job as a housewife and a mother if her head was stuffed with education?

"Please, Mama."

On the other hand, wise men had said that study was the greatest of virtues. For a girl as well as a boy? Even she, the mother of three children, almost a grandmother, yearned to know more. How wonderful to be able to read the Bible and the Prayer Book in Hebrew. How could she say no?

"Go, Rifka," she said reluctantly. "Go and drag the poor geese into the shed before they freeze to death. Aunt Miriam and I will discuss price."

Rifka worked all morning, with Moozeleh trotting back and forth beside her. First, she dragged the coop of excited geese into the already crowded shed. Kvetcher, the rooster, flapped down from the rafters and strutted around the coop, clucking a furious protest against the new tenants. Robbeh, the speckled hen, fluttered around anxiously. Moozeleh sniffed too closely at the long-necked intruders and got her nose nipped.

Rifka piled sacks of flour on top of each other, stacked firewood in a shaky tower, and rehung strings of onion and garlic. The dust rose and terrified mice ran for their lives as Rifka worked. Moozeleh sneezed and retreated to the yard for a nap.

Mama came to help. "Ach," she panted as they struggled to move a sack of potatoes, "if Velvl were here the work would be done one-two-three."

Velvl, Rifka's older brother, had been married the year before and lived a day's wagon ride away, in the large town of Belta.

"But I think you miss him even more than I do," Mama noted her daughter's suddenly gloomy face.

"Oh, how I miss him," Rifka thought, picturing tall Velvl with his sandy, wispy beard and twinkling eyes. Her father spent long days hauling wood from the forest and his children had little time with him. It didn't matter so much when they had Velvl. He always made fun of their little problems and pitched in to help with the big ones. She remembered the time Elli had started school, and she — a grown-up ten-year-old — had cried jealously because she couldn't even read. Velvl didn't laugh, he understood, and spent long hours teaching her. "Don't worry, we'll see him soon," Mama said.

"Soon?" Rifka clapped her hands and made a cloud of dust. "When? Why?"

"Be patient," Mama smiled. "You'll know soon enough."

At last, the work was done. Rifka treated the geese and chickens to a few handfuls of corn as a housewarming present.

Swinging a wooden pail, Rifka and Moozeleh trudged through town to the water hole on the river. Her head was buzzing with ideas. I'll ask Reb Nissen, the butcher, how much I could get for my geese. And then I'll ask Shayndel how much a geography book with colored maps would cost — like the one she told me about. And then I'll need a Russian grammar and a history....

Ice had formed over the water hole. Rifka hacked at it while Moozeleh nosed around in the snow for something to eat. Surely some skater might have left half a boiled potato or a crumb of cheese.

There was a whoosh of runners as Hirsh the drayman drove his sleigh across the bridge.

Rifka stopped and watched him disappear. In a few hours,

the sleigh would be unloading its passengers and cargo in Belta, where Velvl and Fraydeh lived. If it kept going on and on across Russia, through a hundred villages like Savran and many, many farms and huge, dark forests, it would finally reach the end of Russia. On the other side would be another country. Maybe Roumania. And after Roumania would surely come Western Europe. She recited the strange names: France, England, Holland. And after that, the great, heaving Atlantic Ocean — so big that no one could see the opposite side. If she could travel on a big boat for days and nights, she would reach the strange land called America.

Such a big world to think about. And a person could start to see it all by just jumping on Hirsh's sleigh. She pulled her shoulders back and felt laughter rising up inside her until it caught her breath. That whole exciting world was out there, and she, Rifka, would surely see it someday. First she would work hard with Shayndel, and buy books and get high grades on her examination.

But, at the thought of Shyndel, Rifka began to simmer down. She looked uneasily across at the bridge. There were no dark figures standing close together in the shadows today. Only the pale shape of her friend Moozeleh moved about. As she watched, the goat strolled out into the sunshine, munching on the corner of a crumpled piece of paper.

Rifka dropped the rock and slowly stood up. Hadn't Shayndel and the young man been looking at a piece of paper? She crept toward the unsuspecting Moozeleh whose beard was wagging as she chewed. Rifka pounced on the goat, wrapped one arm around her neck, and tried to force her mouth open. Moozeleh jerked loose indignantly, knocked Rifka off her feet on the slippery ice and clattered away up the river bank.

She squirmed upright and smoothed out the scrap of paper

she had managed to snatch from Moozeleh. There were only a few disconnected words left to read in large Russian print. The rest was now a warm, wet mush in the goat's mouth.

"Peasants and workers must fight for..." she read slowly, sounding out the syllables, "end the tyrant's rul...," Finally she deciphered, "...our revolutionary struggle."

Thinking very hard, Rifka finished chipping the hole. On her way back home, icy water splashed from the bucket, but she hardly noticed. She had heard such words before in a hushed whisper. The grownups, speaking softly over a shared newspaper, would use them, and then look anxiously across at the children. These were terrible words, just like secret police, prison, exile... death.

She felt the scrap of paper in her pocket, took a deep breath and decided, "I'll ask Shayndel today."

It was long past lunch time when the teacher hurried in, breathless. Her cheeks and the tip of her nose were red from the cold and her brown eyes sparkled.

"Straftsvoytyeh, good afternoon," she said gaily in Russian to Mama and Rifka.

"Good day to you, Shayndel," Mama answered in Yiddish. She retreated to sit beside the stove and mend Elli's much-patched trousers.

"She's acting as if nothing has happened," Rifka thought, as Shayndel shook the snow from her glossy braids and folded her scarf.

"Why are you watching me?" Shayndel asked.

"I—uh—oh, nothing," Rifka stuttered, suddenly finding that she didn't want to ask about the young man, or the chewed paper, or the gray package, or anything.

With relief, she settled down to a stiff arithmetic drill.

Then they went on to geography. Shayndel drew rough maps to show the places of the various countries of Europe and their major cities. Someplace deep in the geography of the European continent, Rifka forgot Shayndel's mysterious meeting under the bridge and thought no more about it.

They worked hard, going on to Bible reading and Hebrew grammar. Finally, as the shadows were growing long in the kitchen, Rifka worked at twisting her tongue around the difficult Russian sounds, so different from her native Yiddish.

Mama had already filled and lit the kerosene lamp when Shayndel leaned back and closed the book.

"That's enough for today, Rifkalleh," she said, "you're learning so fast that you'll soon catch up with me."

Rifka grinned happily, hoping Mama had heard.

"But time is getting short, and I don't know how we're going to get the books you need for the high school examination." Shayndel shook her head sadly.

Rifka jumped up. "Come, look in the shed," she said. "I have a surprise!"

The geese poked their heads out of the coop as the door squeaked open. Moozeleh came to nuzzle Rifka's hand. The residents of the shed were ready to eat again.

"Just one more minute," Rifka promised them. Proudly, she told Shayndel how she had gotten the geese from Aunt Miriam and worked to make room for them.

"And now," she said excitedly, "I'll have money for books and I'll be able to study even harder, and I'll surely pass the examination."

Shayndel didn't answer, just stood there, crumpling bits of straw between her fingers. At last she said carefully, "You mustn't put your hopes too high. Sometimes even when a student is very good he may not pass the exam."

"Why not?"

"There are quotas."

"Quotas?"

"A quota is a number — the number of Jews who will be allowed to enter high school. A hundred Jewish students may answer every question correctly, but if there's a quota of ten — only ten will be allowed to pass."

"That's not fair," Rifka protested.

"Many things are not fair in our Russia," Shayndel said and turned to go. Suddenly, she turned back, almost tripping over Moozeleh who had followed on her heels.

"Rifka, now that you've made some room here, do you think you could keep a package for me for a little while?"

"Sure, I'll ask Mama."

"Oh, don't bother her about it — it's nothing important — just papers," Shayndel said, blushing a bright pink and staring down at her boots. "We can tuck it right in here behind the firewood."

The cold of the shed prickled through Rifka's body, like a warning. No, she thought, I can't.

Shayndel looked up. Her eyes, usually crinkly and smiling, were pleading. "All right?"

Rifka nodded.

With a quick "thank you," Shayndel was gone.

"Quotas, revolution, tyrants, packages," Rifka mumbled to herself as she tossed in bed.

"What did you say?" Elli asked sleepily.

"I wish Velvl were here, I have so much to ask him."

"You make me tired with all your dumb questions," he yawned. "Good night."

THREE

Aunt Rifka and Uncle Elli

"Hey, Rifkalleh, come here! I have a letter for your mother and father," Hirsh bellowed and waved to her as he wiped down his snorting, stamping horses. He had just arrived in the marketplace with a great jangle of bells and a splatter of slush.

"Rifka, that's the one I was telling you about," he said to the plump, little man who sat on the wagon seat. "Reb Mosheh the woodcutter's daughter. She has a man's head on her shoulders — reads the Bible as though it were a novel for women. A pity she's not a boy."

Rifka and Raizelleh ran over. "A letter?" Rifka asked. She patted the horse's side timidly. To Rifka, the steaming horses and their leather harness smelled of wonderful, faraway places. Raizelleh hid her pink nose in her shawl.

"And it's good news," Hirsh winked and laughed, pulling an envelope out of his pocket and holding it high. "From guess who."

"Who, who?" Rifka jumped, trying to reach it.

"A very old friend. A close, good friend."

"From Belta? Aunt Ettya?"

"No."

"Uncle Solomon?"

"No."

"Who?"

"Get it if you can, and you'll soon see." His bushy mustache wiggled as he laughed and held the letter higher.

"Tch, tch... stop teasing the child," the passenger said, shaking his head.

Rifka suddenly jumped onto the wagon step, and snatched the letter. She ran, with Raizelleh close beside her.

"Thank you, Reb Hirsh," she called back triumphantly.

"Mama, Mama!" They burst into the warm kitchen. "A letter from far away. Hirsh brought it and it's a secret. He wouldn't tell us who gave it to him."

"Where are my onions?" Mama demanded, barely glancing up from the thump, thump, thump of chopping fish. "What did I send you to the market for? Such a short winter day, only three more hours until sundown when the Sabbath starts, and you bother me with Hirsh the driver. Go right back and get those onions!"

"We have a letter." Rifka poked it between her mother's nose and the wooden chopping bowl. Mama stopped work and her eyes opened wide as she wiped her hands on her apron and took it. Letters were not an everyday event in Savran.

"Dear Mother and Father, peace be with you..." Mama read.

"It's from Velvl!" the girls shrieked.

With great happiness, I write to tell you that my wife Fraydeh gave birth to a baby boy today, the eighteenth of Shevat, 5665 — January 24, 1905. They are both well, praise the Lord.

The circumcision will be eight days from now, God

*willing. Tell Rifkalleh that the baby has a potato nose
just like hers, and it yells even louder than Elli.*

Your loving son,
Velvl

"Raizelleh, did you hear that? A baby! That makes me an
aunt and Elli an uncle."

"And I am a grandmother," Mama smiled. Her eyes were
suddenly shiny with tears as she hugged Rifka and Raizalleh.

"Now we have to go to Belta for the circumcision, right,
Mama?"

"We'll see... if all is well. But right now we have to get
ready for the Sabbath. Sabbath comes before anything. I
need the onions first, then you may run and tell the whole
world about the baby. Be back in time to milk Moozeleh and
feed the geese before candle lighting. And Raizelleh, your
mother wants you home soon to help wash your sisters' hair."

"What luck," groaned Raizelleh, "to have two younger sisters. Between them, they have enough hair to stuff a mattress."

"The booths in the marketplace were closing as the shopkeepers hurried to prepare for the Sabbath. Rifka barely
managed to pull some onions from Hannah's sack.

"My big brother Velvl had a baby boy," she told her
happily.

"Well, well, good luck," Hannah nodded. "May he grow
big and strong."

"Hurry, little housewives," Fishkeh the fish peddler sang
out to the nearly empty street. "Your last chance to buy a
lively, fresh jumping fish for the Sabbath."

"Reb Fishkeh," Raizelleh interrupted, "Rifka is a new aunt. Velvl had a baby."

"Good. Another mouth to eat my herring," he laughed. "Buy some fish little housewives..."

After delivering the onions to Mama, they followed the wagon tracks toward the edge of town to Reb Mendl the teacher's house. Elli and the other boys were usually dismissed early on Friday afternoons. They wanted the new uncle to be the first to know the good news. But when they reached the rickety, gray house, they could still hear the sing-song wail of boys reading the Bible.

The girls tiptoed to the window to peek in. At first, they saw only the yellow glow of the fire in the far corner of the room. Then they began to make out the long study table, surrounded by boys — big, little, fat and skinny — all bobbing back and forth over their books. At the head, sat Reb Mendl, the teacher, holding his terrible wooden ruler and sipping a glass of tea.

Raizelleh poked Rifka and pointed. Elli was sitting right below the window, bobbing piously like the others, but one of his hands was busy shuffling a small pile of buttons on the bench beside him.

"Right under Reb Mendl's nose he's playing buttons," Raizelleh murmured admiringly.

"Elli," Rifka whispered, her mouth pressed against a crack in the glass.

Elli swayed and read, while his hand picked a small white button and slid it toward his neighbor.

"Elli, I have a surprise. Pssst," Rifka whispered more loudly.

Pushing his glasses up, Reb Mendl peered suspiciously across the table to the window. His scraggly brows pulled to-

gether over a long, frowning nose as he set his tea down and rose, gripping the ruler. Elli swept the buttons into his pocket without missing a word of reading, and the girls tumbled backward over each other and raced away down the street.

"Am I glad I'm not a boy," Raizelleh panted when they

were safely back in the marketplace. "Reb Mendl's ruler is longer than my arm — I'd hate to be whacked with it."

For once, Rifka agreed. Her own teacher, Shayndel, never even frowned.

"Let's tell Shayndel, too." She pulled Raizelleh across the square and down some steps into the quiet, dimly lit druggist's shop where Shayndel was weighing out powders for her uncle, the druggist.

"Good Sabbath, Shayndel," they greeted her.

"Good Sabbath to you," she answered in surprise. "I hope nobody is sick."

"Oh no, we have good news," Rifka said. "Velvl had a baby."

Shayndel smiled, her dimples dancing. "That's wonderful. Congratulations, Rifkalleh. But girls, you must remember to give credit where credit is due. Velvl's *wife* had the baby. Velvl didn't even have a belly ache. Here, have a peppermint to celebrate."

They ran up the stairs laughing. Rifka looked back to wave goodbye and saw, to her suprise, that Shayndel was leaning forward over the small, brass scale, her face in her hands.

She is so alone, Rifka suddenly realized. "I wish the same good news for you some day, Shayndel," she blurted out.

The young teacher looked up, her face flushed. "No, that's not for me," she said softly, "I have other work to do."

Raizelleh sucked noisily at her peppermint and kicked at clumps of snow as they turned toward her house where two little sisters waited to have their hair washed. She said, "I don't understand your Shayndel. What kind of a dumb thing was that to say? 'It's not for me.' What else is there to do except get married and have babies?"

Rifka didn't answer. Whatever else there was that Shayndel had to do, she didn't seem very happy about it. And if Shayndel was sad... Rifka found her own bright happiness about Velvl's baby and the trip to Belta fading a little.

She stopped at Aunt Miriam's and the cantor's and at Menahem the shoemaker's. Everywhere, black smoke rose from the chimneys into the cold, blue sky, pots stewed and simmered on the stoves and the tables were already set with candlesticks and spread with white cloths. Filled with best wishes and kisses and tastes of chicken soup, she finally started for home and bumped squarely into her father. He was humming a melody into his wavy, brown beard, carrying his clean clothing under his arm and hurrying to the bath house.

"Slow down, little daughter. Remember your new position in life — aunts must be dignified and fat and respectable. And grandfathers are too frail to be bumped into." His eyes, blue like Rifka's, twinkled. "You'd better hurry and help Mama. Moozeleh is climbing the wall, waiting for supper, and half the town will be coming over to wish us well tonight."

By the time the beadle knocked on their shutters and called, "time to light the Sabbath candles," they were ready. The floor gleamed gold with its fresh layer of sand; the oven was sealed with clay to keep the stew warm for Sabbath afternoon, when no fire could be lit; the large tea urn stood full and hot. Mama sat by the candles, wearing her white kerchief and reading in a soft murmur from her Prayer Book while she waited for the men to return from the synagogue. Rifka leaned against the warm bricks of the oven wall, making finger shadows on the whitewashed wall...there was the letter "bet," and a "daled," and a "shin." Her eyes slid to the glass bookcase doors with Papa's precious leather-bound books inside, then to the golden, braided Sabbath bread on the candlelit table. Frost was thick on the windows, but the house was warm with food smells and the joy of the holiday and the joy of Velvl's new son. She hugged her knees and thought, why should Shayndel be sad? Why should anybody be sad?

There was a stamping of feet on the porch.

"Good Sabbath everybody," Papa called, "I've brought a guest from the synagogue for supper."

Behind him stood Elli and the round, little man from Hirsh's wagon.

"This is Reb Berl of Malin, a travelling fixer of watches and clocks."

Mama greeted the guest, and quickly added a little water to the soup. When they settled around the table, Rifka and Elli watched the stranger curiously. Other travelling "fixers" — tinsmiths, knife sharpeners, tailors — who shared their Sabbath meals were lean and tattered. But this clock-fixer had a round, well-fed look. He smacked his lips over the beet soup with potatoes, fish cakes and chicken. By the time they reached the stewed fruit, Reb Berl was full enough to carry on a conversation.

"So — you older son lives in Belta."

"Yes, a fine modern town, much better than our little Savran," Papa said proudly.

"Modern? Yes. Fine? I'm not so sure."

"Why, what's wrong with Belta?" Papa protested, "There are factories, brick houses, a modern railroad station."

"True, true, modern enough. Right up to the latest fashion

of 1905," said Reb Berl. "Some houses have water drawn right out of the wall, from pipes, instead of keeping a full barrel in the kitchen. And the streets are crowded with carriages, and even horseless carriages."

The family nodded. They had seen these wonders on their visits.

"But some say it's too modern." He stopped to suck some chicken from his tooth. "Some say that in Belta and the other big towns there is too much modern-ness, too much wildness. Children don't obey parents, the eggs know more than the chickens, and terrible things are happening."

"What terrible things?" Papa asked.

The guest looked around, leaned forward, and spoke in a loud whisper.

"Young people, boys and girls, are forming groups and plotting together to kill people, to make revolutions, to overthrow the government! Of course, in a little town like Savran, you wouldn't know of such things."

"We have our revolutionaries here, too," Mama began.

"Tch, tch. Is that so?" Reb Berl waited for her to continue, but Papa quickly put his hand on hers and interrupted. "It's a bad business," he said. "If they're caught they'll rot in chains for talking against the government."

"Not just they, but their mothers and fathers and sisters and brothers!" The stranger shook his finger under Papa's nose. "Last week, the police tore the door of Eliahu the herring merchant from its hinges, rushed down to his cellar and dug up two sacks of pamphlets buried under the floor — pamphlets demanding that the workers join together, break into the police barracks, and steal guns to use in an armed revolution."

He looked around at his silent audience and continued,

"They also found three guns wrapped in potato sacks."

"Guns!" Mama gasped and her spoon clattered into her dish.

"Eliahu's two sons were immediately arrested. They confessed that they, only they, had buried the sacks. But that didn't help. The father and mother and two younger brothers were also arrested, and at this moment they're being held in prison and questioned. And if they live through that, they'll all be sent to prison camp in the far north where the snow never melts."

Satisfied with their breathless attention, Reb Berl took a last spoonful of prunes and wiped his mouth. "Too modern," he sighed and leaned back, gently rubbing his belly. "But, never mind, why am I telling you these things? It's a happy time for you, with a new grandson, and I'm giving you a headache with this politics nonsense. Please, a glass of tea, my throat is dry."

Papa looked at Mama's pale face as she brought in the tea. "Let's welcome the Sabbath with joy," he said and began to sing softly, "Peace be with you, angels of peace, angels from high above...."

The stranger joined in enthusiastically and so did Elli. But Rifka's voice seemed stuck in her throat and her hand shook so that she spilled tea on the tablecloth.

Soon Raizelleh's mother and father knocked on the door, and then Menahem the shoemaker and Aunt Miriam and others. The room grew crowded and warm. Mama's cheeks were rosy as she poured tea. Rifka and Elli were busy carrying glasses, putting away coats, and getting pinched and hugged. But Rifka's eye kept straying to the kitchen door leading to the shed. In there, behind the cages of geese, behind the piled up firewood, lay Shayndel's gray package. What could be in it? Pamphlets, guns... who knows? And what if the wood slipped down? What if the police came? Poor Mama and Papa, and even Elli — what terrible danger was she getting them into? They sat smiling, talking gaily, drinking tea... if they only knew.

"Rifkalleh." Her mother's voice startled her. "Please get some more jam from the top shelf in the kitchen."

She went past the shed door, pulled a chair over and climbed to reach the high shelf. Suddenly she heard the squeak of hinges behind her. Spinning around, she saw the shed door opening.

"Aaaaah," she gasped involuntarily, mouth open, as Reb Berl the clock fixer appeared in the doorway, wiping his forehead with a large handkerchief.

"What is it, girl?" he smiled. "You look as if you've seen the devil."

"Why... w-what were you d-doing in the shed?" she stuttered.

"It's so warm in here, I stepped out to cool off. That's a fine batch of geese you have in there." He reached up to steady her. "Calm yourself, child. Why are you shivering? Better get yourself some hot tea."

FOUR

Hello and Goodbye

Elli's knees made bumps in the bear robe as he drummed on the floor of the sleigh. "Mmeee..ee..ee" he whinnied, just loud enough to hear himself above the whooshing of the runners and the creaking of the sleigh.

Rifka stretched her tongue to lick snow from her cheeks. She was sure there was an icicle hanging from her nose, but her tongue couldn't reach that far and it was too cold to pull her hands out from under the warm fur. New showers of ice and snow sprayed into their faces with each lurch of the rushing sleigh. "To Belta, to Belta, to Belta.." the horse's hooves drummed on the rutted snow of the road.

"To Velvl, to Velvl, to Velvl..." she sang and tried to imagine whether her brother would have changed. Would he be fatter and duller now that he was a father, ready to pinch cheeks but not to listen or play? No, not Velvl — he would always be Velvl. He would find time to talk to her about Shayndel and the package.

The sky brightened slowly to a pale silvery blue and then to a rising, glowing gold. They rushed past shimmering fields and snowladen houses. Rifka's eyes burned with melting snow. She squeezed them shut, tucked the robe under her chin, and fell asleep.

"Welcome to Belta! Wake up lazy bones."

The sled seat had stopped bouncing. There was a hubbub of voices and the stamping and snorting of horses. Rifka blinked up at a gleaming noon sun. The sled stood in front of a two-story house with a balcony, a rich man's house like Reb Leib's in Savran. Velvl had married well. Suddenly two big, warm hands seized her waist and Rifka felt herself flying through the air.

"Aiyeee!" she screeched.

Velvl's curly beard tickled her face and she was squeezed breathless in a great bear hug.

"Hoo-ha," he exclaimed, setting her down on the ground beside the sleigh, "you must have gained twenty pounds since the last time I lifted you. But you're still a little skinny for an aunt. Wait till you see your new nephew!"

His eyes sparkled and his earlocks bobbed in the breeze just the way they used to.

"Hey Velvl," she laughed with relief, "you don't look like a proper father, either."

But Velvl had already turned to hoist Elli down and to greet his mother and father and lead them all into his father-in-law's house. Reb Sender, his wife, and Zissel the maid were waiting with tea and food and basins of steaming water to wash up before the great event of the day, the *bris milah*, the circumcision ceremony.

Mama warned Elli about not jumping, not running, not crawling into or under things, not eating like a pig, but eating enough that he wouldn't have to be a pig later on, not yelling... "Is it all right if I breathe?" he had asked sulkily.

Guests were already gathering in the dining room downstairs when Velvl's mother-in-law, splendid in a tall, glossy brown wig and a rustling black dress, led them to see the baby. They went past the crowded dining room and Elli sniffed wistfully at the long table piled with honey cake, sponge cake, strudel, and bottles of golden brandy and red wine.

"Later," Mama whispered and pulled him along.

Velvl was waiting in the doorway, beaming proudly. "Come in, come in." He drew them into a dimly lit bedroom. The curtains were drawn and the air seemed padded, velvety thick.

"Where's the baby? I can't see anything." Rifka whispered, clutching Mama's arm.

"It's dark because the windows are shuttered and covered to keep out evil spirits. The time before the circumcision is very dangerous for the baby."

"Here we are, Rifkalleh," Fraydeh's voice laughed warmly from the opposite side of the room. A lamp brightened as she turned up the wick. The new mother sat propped up in bed on a pile of pillows, with the baby beside her.

"Mazel tov... a long life... much joy," they hugged and kissed Fraydeh and then gathered around to look at the most important person in the room — the newcomer.

A tiny, worried red face peeped up at them out of its wide brimmed, lace cap. The baby's eyes were round and blue-gray.

"He has Rifka's potato nose, just like Velvl wrote," Elli said.

At that, the little face wrinkled up like a prune and the toothless mouth opened in an indignant yowl. Everybody laughed, even Rifka.

"No evil should harm him," Mama marvelled, "he has a wonderful pair of lungs."

"Of course. He'll be a cantor when he grows up," the other grandmother declared. "No evil eye. Ptooey, ptooey, ptooey," she spat over her shoulder to ward off the evil eye.

When the family reached the dining room the *mohel*, the circumcizor, was waiting. There was barely enough time for Rifka and Elli to be pinched on the cheeks and told how big they had grown by their Belta relatives when a meowing wail was heard from the hall.

"Aha, sha, be quiet," the guests smiled. "The guest of honor is coming."

The wailing grew louder.

"Tch, tch, bless him. Such lungs." Mama clucked in admiration, just as Aunt Etya, the godmother, appeared in the doorway holding the baby on an embroidered pillow.

The guests rose and called out together, "Blessed be he who comes."

The baby was handed to the godfather. He placed him in the broad lap of Uncle Solomon, who was sitting in a special high-backed chair, the chair of Elijah, which was used by the community only for circumcisions.

"I am ready to carry out God's commandment to circumcize my son, as it is written in the Bible," Velvl said, looking pale and sober.

The *mohel* began to recite the prayers before the ceremony.

"Where's Fraydeh?" Rifka whispered. "She's missing everything."

"The mother never comes," Mama whispered back. "It would curdle her milk. Shhh."

There was a sudden howl from the baby as the cut was quickly made, and just as quickly he quieted down and began to suck on a bit of gauze soaked in wine that the *mohel* held to his lips.

"Our God, God of our fathers, preserve this child, his father and his mother," the *mohel* continued, "and let his name be called in Israel — Joseph, the son of Velvl. Let the father rejoice."

The guests responded together, "As he has entered the Covenant, so may he enter into the study of the Bible, the marriage canopy, and a life of good deeds."

"Amen! Mazel Tov!" The guests burst out, as Joseph, the son of Velvl, the newest, smallest member of God's covenant with the Jewish people, was carried back to his mother.

"He doesn't look like a Joseph," Elli said. "Josephs are big and have beards, like Joseph the blacksmith."

"We'll call him Yosselleh until he grows up," Mama answered.

Reb Sender raised his glass high in a toast to Velvl. "May you have pleasure in your children, and your children's children, and your children's children's children." He was followed by Papa's toast, and Velvl's, and Uncle Solomon's, and more, and more. The covenant was celebrated with wine, brandy, cake, joy, and singing as the sun sank in the clear winter sky.

Rifka stuffed herself with cake until her pink dress strained at each button. Then she circled around the men, trying to catch Velvl's eye. He was flushed and singing, busy being a proud, new father. Oh, well, she thought, there's still tomorrow.

"Up, up, up." Rifka forced her eyes open at the sound of Mama's voice.

The curtains were drawn wide and a glittering, cold sun

flooded the room. Elli was already up, spluttering and protesting as Mama gripped his shirt collar firmly and helped
him scrub up to his elbows.

"Get up, Rifkalleh," she called over her shoulder. "Wash
and get dressed and I'll help you braid your hair. Today we
all have to look specially beautiful; we're going to have a picture taken."

"Rifkalleh would have to spend all her goose money and
buy a brand new face before she could be beautiful," Elli
hooted, running for the door.

Rifka jumped out of bed and caught him with a kick that
sent him sprawling into the hall.

"Shame on you," Mama scolded, "are you a peasant girl to
kick like that?"

But this wasn't Mama's crackling, scolding voice. Rifka
looked at her sharply. Her eyes were red and there were dark
circles under them. Why, she's been crying, Rifka thought in
surprise. Maybe it's happy crying because she's a grandmother now.

"Mama, why are we taking a picture and why were you..."
she began.

Mama was already on her way out, calling back, "Everybody is done already. Hurry down for breakfast and I'll help
you with your hair afterwards."

When Rifka reached the kitchen, Elli was already seated at
the table, dunking bread in warm milk. Zissel the maid
bustled around, sweeping, straightening, and scolding them
to hurry so she could begin preparing lunch.

"Do people eat all day long in Belta?" Elli asked.

"Country bumpkins," she sniffed scornfully. "Don't ask silly
questions. Just finish, and then — out!"

There was a chuckle from the doorway

"If they're country bumpkins, then I must be too." Velvl came in brushing sparkles of snow from his beard. His cheeks and nose were red from the brisk walk home from morning prayers.

"Oy, another one under my feet. If there's no lunch today, it won't be my fault." Zissel threw up her hands and stamped off to the cellar.

"Poor Zissel. She'll be happy when this week is over." Velvl shook his head. "It's been so busy I haven't even had a chance to talk to you both. I want all the news from home. How are your studies going, Rifkalleh? And Elli, is Reb Mendl whacking you as hard as he used to? Has the roof started leaking where I fixed it last winter..."

"Oh Velvl!" Rifka interrupted and leaned over to hug him. "I've been waiting and waiting. There's so much I have to tell you about and ask you about. Everything is so mixed up."

"Me too! Me first! I'm younger," Elli yelled.

"Elli, keep quiet. Go away. This is very important."

"So is mine!"

"Wait a minute," Velvl laughed and put a hand over each mouth. "I have something very important to tell both of you, too. Let me talk first."

Disappointed, Rifka held back her tumbling words and waited.

"This is going to surprise you, but Fraydeh and I have been thinking about it for a long time," he said and then stopped. He curled a bit of beard around his forefinger, took a deep breath, and began again.

"Well, we decided, Fraydeh and I decided, that we don't want to live in Russia anymore."

Rifka gasped.

"We want to make a better life for ourselves and our baby. We decided that I will go to America. I'll get a job, and I'll work hard, and very, very soon I'll earn enough money to send for Fraydeh and Yosselleh."

"But Velvl, you can't go. That's too far away. We'll never see you again. It's way across the Atlantic Ocean." Rifka's voice choked up with tears.

"It's not so far, Rifkalleh. Frumeh the dressmaker and Uncle Pinyeh and other people from Savran are there already."

"Wow — that's terrific! America! Hurray!" Elli jumped up and smacked Velvl's shoulder excitedly. "Hey, watch out for the Indians over there. They'll slice the scalp right off your head — swoosh! I know because Zev told me. And his uncle from Odessa told him."

"I'm glad you warned me, Elli," Velvl grinned. "I'll fool those Indians. I'll never take my hat off, even in bed."

"Why should you go?" Rifka asked, desperately. "It's so fine here in Reb Sender's house. There's a pantry full of food and a silver samovar for tea and a great big house of study full of books, and you can work in Reb Sender's store to earn a living... and you have a new baby and Fraydeh... and... and... I need you."

"Rifkalleh, a worm that lives in horseradish thinks the horseradish is sweet. But I'm not a worm. I know that Russia is a bitter place for Jews. I want to live in a country where I'll be able to walk down the street with my wife and my son and be afraid of nobody. Nobody! I want to be free to travel to the farthest corner of the land, not to be penned up in one corner like a goose waiting for the butcher. I want my children to be welcome in school, not shut out by quotas, and I don't want to live in fear and lock my shutters and wait for a pogrom after every Christian holiday."

Rifka turned away and hid her face in her arms.

"Little sister," he put his hands on her shoulders, "I'm not deserting you. It's not just for me that I'm going. It's for you and Elli and Mama and Papa, too. I'll work hard, I promise. I'll earn enough money to bring you all to America."

"Come." He tugged playfully at her braid. "Come into the dining room and I'll show you my ship's ticket. It's nothing but a piece of paper and yet a person can ride halfway around the world with it. Come on."

She kept her head down, stiff with misery, ignoring him until he gave up and moved away. She heard the footsteps as he and Elli left the kitchen. Then the flood of tears burst out. She sobbed and hiccupped and dripped all over her bread and milk and her long pink sleeves. How could he do this? How could he leave when she needed him so much?

Many miserable minutes later, Rifka felt her hair being stroked gently.

"Red eyes and a red nose. Every time Velvl looks at our family picture, that's what he'll see," a soft voice murmured.

Rifka sniffed and peered up through a teary blur to see Fraydeh beside her. She was all dressed up in a blue silk dress with a white lace collar and, as she leaned over Rifka, her earrings dangled and gleamed. But Fraydeh's eyes were red, just as Mama's eyes had been that morning.

"Fraydeh, how can you let him go?" she cried.

"I don't want to," Fraydeh answered. "I must. I've thought and thought about it. I know how lonely I'll be. I'll watch the baby grow and I'll want to share every beautiful new thing with Velvl. When the baby's first tooth comes in, and when he says 'Mama', and when he takes his first step, I won't be able to turn and laugh with Velvl. I'll have to sit down and write a letter. And the letter will wander for weeks and weeks, in and out of mail wagons and across the rivers and oceans until it reaches him. He'll be a stranger to his own son.''

She pulled a handkerchief out of her sleeve and blew her nose, looked at Rifka who was crying again, and gave her a clean corner to blow on.

"But we're not happy here," she continued, "We live on a volcano. Last Easter, the peasants roamed through the streets and tore apart my father's store, and bloodied up every Jew they found on the street. For three whole days we hid in the attic like cowards and prayed they wouldn't break into our house. Velvl and I want to be free and America is a free land. And Rifkalleh, the wonderful thing is that America wants us! We just have to work hard and it will give us everything we could dream of — schools, synagogues, a piece of land to plant a garden. It's hard to believe — there are even Jewish policemen in America!

"So I must be patient and wait. And you have to be patient too." She took a deep breath. "Now let's wash our faces in cold water, and I'll braid your hair with blue satin ribbons. We're going to the photographer to take a family picture for Velvl to take with him. We don't want him to forget us." Fraydeh laughed.

Zissel thumped up the steps and flung open the kitchen door. She carried a huge bowl full of pickled cucumbers, watermelon, and tomatoes and a loaf of bread under each arm.

"Still eating?" she cried. "No, they're not eating any

more — now they're crying!" She rolled her eyes upward and complained loudly, "Never have I seen so much crying for such a happy occasion. It's an upside down world these days. Now — out of my kitchen, Fraydeh. You may be a big mother now, but that doesn't impress me. I knew you when you were in diapers, so do as you're told!"

Fraydeh and Rifka grabbed hands and ran.

FIVE

Purim Thieves

"The tall one with the fuzzy brown beard is my brother Velvl — he's in America now. And right next to him is his wife Fraydeh. Here's Mama and Papa — I bet you never saw them dressed up so fancy. And over here is Rifkalleh. I don't know why they let her hold the baby instead of me.

"And here's me. My eyes are crossed because there was this fly who kept zooming around my head, and he landed on my nose and just then — click — the photographer took the picture."

"But I don't see him. Where's the fly?" Zev asked.

Both boys were sprawled on their elbows across the dining room table studying the new family photograph.

"One second before the click, I shot my tongue up, dragged that fly down into my mouth and swallowed him."

"You did not! Flies aren't Kosher," Zev protested.

Elli began to laugh.

"Liar!" Zev shoved Elli's elbow to make him collapse.

"Children, out of the dining room," Mama called from the kitchen. "Come in here and make yourselves useful. We need walnuts shelled for the honey cake, and prunes have to be chopped for hamentashen. In two days, it will be Purim. Thank heavens, we're finally seeing the end of the winter.

Where is that Rifka? I sent her to the druggist for saffron for Purim bread an hour ago."

"Everything is different in America," Elli continued at the kitchen table as he and Zev cracked nuts. "Everybody has big coaches with six horses — as big as the Czar's. People even have two fur coats, a fox coat for the Sabbath, and a bear coat for workdays. And they eat honey cake and white rolls and fried goose even on weekdays."

"Velvl, too?"

"Well, maybe not Velvl. He's saving his money to send us all ship's tickets to come to America."

"For all of you? It would take a million years to save that much money. You'd be leaning on a cane and tripping on your beard by then."

"Mama," Elli appealed, "How long will it take Velvl to save enough money to bring us all to America?"

"What nonsense you talk! Grownups chew and children spit

out. Velvl will be lucky if he earns enough to bring his wife and child to America. Just stop dreaming and," she leaned across and smacked his hand, "stop eating the nuts. There'll be nothing left to bake with."

"I wish I could earn some money to help him," Elli said, "So I could get there faster."

Mama opened the oven door. A sweet, cinnamon smell filled the kitchen as she pulled out a pan of sugar cookies, set it down, and quickly pushed in a pan of nut cookies. She counted the cookies and thought out loud. "Two more pans and I'll have enough for *shalah manos*, the dishes of Purim gifts. I'll hunt up a ruble's worth of coins to pay the boys who deliver the dishes, and I think I'll put a few almonds on each dish..."

Zev poked Elli. "A whole ruble," he whispered.

"A whole ruble," Elli repeated slowly and grinned.

"Mama!" he exclaimed, "I can deliver your Purim plates, and then I'll save the ruble for my ship's ticket, and then Velvl won't have to work so hard."

"Tickets, tickets, tickets! Stop this ticket nonsense!" Mama slammed down the rolling pin. "We're not going to America. We're going to the synagogue to hear the Purim story, and then we're going to start preparing for Passover and after that for Shavuos. Savran is our home and we can be good Jews and serve God in Savran even better that we could in America where people work on the Sabbath and shave off their beards and earlocks!

"Now stop bothering me with your tickets and your rubles. Go and find Rifka and send her home with the saffron."

"What got into Mama?" Elli wondered as he and Zev

jumped from frozen clump to frozen clump of grass, avoiding the puddles of mud caused by the spring thaw.

"Who knows?" Zev shrugged. "But don't worry. Nag her. Usually you can wear them down until they give in."

Rifka stood near the druggist's counter, clutching the cup of yellow saffron. Her face was hot with anger at Shayndel's words.

"Velvl is running away!" Shaydel whispered fiercely. "If he wanted freedom, he should have stayed here to fight for it. That's what my comrades and I are doing, Jews and Christians, we're all working together. And you'll see, one day very soon we'll win our fight and we'll have a constitution and free elections and people won't be dragged off to prison."

"And the attacks against Jews, the pogroms?"

"Of course, there won't be any more pogroms, Rifka. People only attack Jews because they're miserable and hungry and they need somebody to blame for all their troubles. After we force the Czar to give us a constitution, everybody will have equal rights and nobody will be hungry. It'll be beautiful, you'll see. And Velvl could be helping, but instead he ran away."

"That can't be right," Rifka said stubbornly. "Velvl would never run away. He's the best, sweetest, smartest person I know, and if he went to America, then it was the right thing to do."

"Oh Rifkalleh," Shayndel patted her hand. "I'm not insulting him. He just didn't know the truth. He never learned about socialism. But you're different. You want a real education." Her voice got even softer. "I'm going to give you something to read that will explain about the revolution. But don't let anybody else see it."

She reached among the boxes and jars of medicines and herbs on the shelf behind her.

"Mama and Papa wouldn't let me," Rifka said.

Shayndel tuned back, smiling, and pushed a small black book into Rifka's hands. "You don't have to tell your Mama and Papa everything."

On the eve of Purim, the old synagogue shook and the dust of centuries rose into the air as Rifka, Raizelleh, Elli, Zev, and the other children stamped their feet and beat their tin noisemakers. They listened to the story of beautiful Queen Esther and her wise cousin Mordecai who saved the Jews from the wicked Prime Minister Haman. Every time Haman's name was mentioned, the roof nearly lifted with the happy pandemonium. The red velvet curtain in front of the Ark billowed as if the Torah scrolls inside were laughing, too. When Reb Mendl the teacher hushed the children, they ignored him brazenly. On Purim, they could do anything — almost.

Breakfast on Purim morning was a feast of hamentashen, three-cornered pastries filled with prunes and poppyseeds, a feast that even the Czar would envy — *his* mother couldn't make hamentashen.

When Fanya, the peasant neighbor who lit their stove on the Sabbath, came in to borrow an egg, Mama insisted she try a hamentash, too.

"Mmmm... you make good things," Fanya said. "I like your white Sabbath bread and your Purim cakes. We have

nice things, too. At Easter, we parade with willow branches
and we color eggs and make a wonderful paska of white
cheese."

"That's funny. We cut branches too — at Shavuos and
Sukkos," Rifka said.

Mama smiled.

Elli could hardly wait for Fanya to leave so he could continue his campaign.

"Maaaaa."

"You're maa-ing like Moozeleh. Speak!"

"Ma, please, can't I deliver the Purim dishes for you?"

"Again?" She threw up her hands. "You could wheedle the
eggs out from under a chicken. All right, all right."

She turned to the shelf over the water barrel where covered
dishes were lined up. "Now, this dish goes to Zev's mother:
two sugar cookies, one square of fruit cake, two honey balls, a
prune tart, and some almonds. Carry it carefully, watch out
for the mud, and don't slip.

"Rifkalleh, hold Moozeleh, don't let her out. She's so
pregnant she can barely get through the gate, but she's still
fast enough to snatch a cookie from under Elli's nose."

Taking small, careful steps and pressing the dish against
his stomach, Elli stepped off the porch and started down the
street.

"Don't forget to wish Zev's mother a happy holiday and
many more, and say 'thank you' when she gives you two
groschen," Mama called after him.

"Happy holiday, thank you, watch out for mud, happy
holiday, thank you, watch out for mud, happy holiday..."
Elli repeated to himself, as he walked toward the
marketplace.

"Hey, Elli!" Zev's voice stopped him short. He also held a dish covered with a white napkin pressed against his stomach.

"Are you going to my house?"

Elli nodded. "And are you going to mine?"

"Yes, we're both earning money today. Hurray for Purim! Put your dish down and rest a minute. I have to get a pebble out of my shoe."

They put their dishes down on the least muddy barrel and talked for awhile. Zev said, "Let's see what your mother is sending to my mother."

"All right," Elli agreed, "if you let me see what your mother is sending to my mother."

They lifted their white napkins and compared. It was an amazing mathematical triumph, as if the two women had measured and weighed and calculated to the last ounce of swetness and flavor and came out exactly even.

"My two sugar cookies match your two nut cookies."

"And my apple tart matches your fruit cake."

"And my two honey balls match your big hamentash."

"And your prune tart matches my strudel."

"And your four walnuts match my four almonds."

"Perfect!" Zev said and gulped.

"Exactly perfect," said Elli, licking his lips.

"Well," he covered the dish, "I'd better go."

Then both at the same time began, "Would it matter..." and both stopped and began laughing.

Zev looked around and said, "Now look, if I take one of your nut cookies and you take one of my sugar cookies we'll still be even. Right?"

"Right. Let's."

"Your mother makes good cookies."

"So does yours, but I'd love to try that strudel."

"All right, then I'll have your prune tart and we'll still be even."

Next, they traded a honey ball for half a hamentash, evened up the nuts and generously tossed one almond and one walnut to the gaunt, ownerless billy goat who wandered through town snatching a bite wherever he could. Then, feeling good about the world, the holiday and each other, they went their separate ways.

Zev's mother, Golda, opened the door and smiled at the messenger.

"I have a Purim gift for you from my mother and she wishes you and your family a happy holiday and many more and thank you." Elli rattled it all off in a breathless rush.

"The same to you and your family," said Golda, uncovering the dish. The she gasped and her smile vanished.

"I really didn't think times were so bad for Reb Mosheh that your mother would have to send half a hamentash," she said stiffly and fumbled in her apron for a penny.

"Uh, uh, t-t-trees grow pretty slow," Elli stammered a reply, snatched his penny and ran.

The two friends passed each other in the marketplace several times that Purim day, but they didn't stop to compare dishes again.

After afternoon prayers, Mama set glasses on the table along with dishes of Purim treats which had come from all over town. Neighbors would be dropping in for a happy Purim drink. It wasn't often that the people of Savran had a chance to celebrate a victory over a tyrant, and even though Haman had been dead for fourteen hundred years, they made the most of it.

Papa came home with rosy cheeks and sparkling eyes, humming a tune. He had already made a few stops in honor of the holiday. He helped Elli count out his earnings, helped Mama pour the cherry wine and then settled down to chat and sing with the visitors.

When Mama began to light the kerosene lamps, the men rose to go to evening prayers. Papa suddenly remarked, "Strange that Chayim didn't drop in this afternoon the way he does every year."

"Very strange. Did you quarrel with him?" Mama asked.

"Heaven forbid. Why would I quarrel with such an old friend?"

"If you didn't quarrel with Chayim the cloth merchant, and I certainly didn't quarrel with Chayim the cloth merchant's wife, then why did she send us such a stingy dish of Purim treats? And I wasted a whole beautiful dishful on such a one!"

Mama's voice was indignant and loud enough that Rifka could hear it out in the storage room where she crouched over the small black book by candlelight. She stuck her fingers in her ears and read the line again, "From each according to his ability, to each according to his need." Her brows pulled together and she sat puzzling.

Papa chose the long way around through the twilight streets to pass the cloth merchant's house. He saw no sense in prolonging a quarrel, if there was a quarrel.

"Good evening to you, Chayim," he called, catching sight of Zev's father ahead.

"Brrmm," grunted the cloth merchant and walked faster.

Papa tried again. "I was sorry you didn't stop in for a sip of wine for Purim."

"I'll bet," Chayim spat over his shoulder, clapped a hand on his hat, and broke into a half trot.

Papa hoisted up his long coat and hurried to catch up. "How is your wife and the children?"

"Stop bothering me," Chayim panted. "Your wife clearly wants to pick a fight with my wife. If you really want to know how she is tell your wife to go and ask her."

He overtook Fishkeh the fish seller, also on his way to the synagogue, and hurried past him.

"Is there a fire?" Fishkeh yelled. "Is somebody sick?"

Next Papa rushed past.

"Somebody must be sick. Whoa!" called Fishkeh. "Reb Mosheh, is your little Elli sick? I saw him and Zev stuffing themselves from their Purim dishes in the marketplace this morning."

Zev's father slowed down and stopped. Papa slid to a halt right behind him and they both turned to Fishkeh.

"My Zev?"

"My Elli?"

The two men looked at each other with sudden understanding, smiled, began to chuckle, burst out laughing, and then, clapping each other on the back, walked side by side to evening prayers.

Elli and Zev met again later that evening. Elli was on his way to apologize to Zev's mother and Zev was to do the same with Elli's mother.

"The only thing that saved us was that it's Purim. And on Purim any trick is all right. Otherwise — wow!" Zev rolled his eyes and rubbed his rear.

"I still don't know what they're mad about," Elli complained. "We were fair, we kept it even."

SIX

Moozeleh Does Her Best

Moozeleh the goat was having a bad day. Whichever way she lay, her belly kept bumping and heaving and getting in the way of her legs.

"Meh-eh-eh," she complained to Rifka and Mama, who were sitting on the front steps in the pale spring sunshine, Mama flicking feathers from a chicken and Rifka peeling potatoes.

Rifka threw some peels to her, but for once Moozeleh wasn't hungry. She nosed aimlessly around under the steps, climbed onto the porch and butted Rifka's back for attention, but Mama and Rifka were too busy talking to notice. Seeking a quiet, comfortable place to lie down and ease her troubled belly, Moozeleh slipped in the open front door and settled on a pile of sacks in front of the warm oven wall in the kitchen.

Potatoes thumped into the pot and chicken feathers floated over the fence as the girl and the woman talked.

"I don't know," Rifka shook her head and complained, "the more I study the more mixed up I get."

"You'll just have to work harder. I can't help you with Hebrew grammar or Russian or geography."

"No, no! It's not grammar or geography, it's ideas that I don't understand." She hesitated, not sure she should tell her mother about Shayndel's book, but Mama had stopped plucking feathers and looked at her, waiting.

"Well, for instance, one of my books says, 'From each according to his ability, to each according to his need.' Doesn't that mean that everybody should work as hard as he can?" Rifka continued, forgetting her lapful of potatoes, "A big strong person would do a lot of work and a little, old person would do only a little bit. But then, when they got paid, each of them should get as much money as he needs. So the old person could buy soft, white bread because he has no teeth, or a warm fur coat because he gets cold easily. But the strong, young person who doesn't need much wouldn't get paid as much. Doesn't that sound good?" she finished breathlessly and beamed at her mother.

Mama answered the question with a question. "Why would the strong person work hard if he knew he would get very little pay for it?"

"Just to help," Rifka said, surprised. "To make things better for everybody."

"You're a child," said Mama with a smile and went back to plucking.

With a creaking of the wooden harness and a clank of his pails, old Lazer the water carrier stopped at their gate. He groaned as he leaned one end of the harness on their fence and his wrinkled cheeks seemed to slide into the hole of his toothless mouth.

"Any water today?" he mumbled.

"You see," Rifka whispered, "Why should Lazer be working so hard? Look how tired he is and look at his feet. He has rags wrapped around them."

"Sha, Rifkalleh. Don't shame the man." Mama hushed

her. "Yes, Reb Lazer. Please pour one pail of water into the kitchen barrel." She hunted through her pockets and pulled out a few groschen as Lazer shuffled up the stairs with his heavy pail.

"Groschen!" Rifka scolded. "No wonder he can't buy shoes. Why don't you give him more?"

"I don't have more!" Mama flared up. "We give more to charity than we can really afford. At Passover time, Lazer's family and every other poor family gets matzah and wine. We just helped his daughter with her dowry..."

"That's different," Rifka argued. "Charity is a favor."

They heard the clank of the pail inside and then Lazer's shuffle as he returned.

"Ay, ay Chaykeh," he called from the doorway with a broad, bare gummed smile, "Do you know what's happening in your kitchen?"

Mama jumped up and hurried in. Moozeleh lay on the sacks in front of the oven wall; her bulging side heaved up and down. She bleated wearily and stretched her neck toward Mama. Between her hind legs, two tiny legs had appeared, pushing slowly from the birth canal, moving, growing longer as Mama and Rifka watched. Then a nose and a small head inched out, tucked down against the knobby little knees.

"Meh-eh-eh," bleated Moozeleh shrilly.

"Rifka, get Papa," Mama said urgently. "He's in the marketplace."

"I want to watch," Rifka pleaded.

"Go!"

Rifka went.

By the time she and Papa came home carrying armfuls of hay, Moozeleh lay more quietly. She was breathing calmly and was busy licking a tiny, bony, black and white baby goat tucked against her shaggy body.

"Good little Moozeleh, sweet little Moozeleh," Mama murmured, setting a bowl of warm milk beside her as she stroked her. "Now stop licking your baby for a minute, mothers need strength."

Moozeleh lapped at the milk for a few minutes and then returned to her work of cleaning the new kid. It lay quiet and weary, only its nose wiggled now and then, exploring the strange smells of the new world.

Rifka reached to touch the wet fur but Moozeleh quickly aimed a sharp hind hoof at her hand.

"Moozeleh, this is me," Rifka said indignantly, "your best friend!"

"Leave her be," Papa smiled. "This is an anxious time for her. She trusts only me because I helped her through labor before." She held perfectly still while Papa cut the umbilical cord which tied the kid to its mother.

Suddenly Moozeleh cried out again and began to breathe hard.

"I believe we are going to be twice blessed," said Papa. "Chaykeh, would you set up the samovar for tea? This may take some time."

"Poor Moozeleh," Rifka groaned and felt her own belly ache sympathetically.

The sky sparkled with stars and shouting schoolboys carrying candle lanterns had already made their way home through the muddy streets when Moozeleh finally finished her labor. A second frail kid lay shivering beside her. She let it rest a while and then, as Elli and Rifka watched spellbound,

Moozeleh stood up and nudged each of the little ones who
were huddled together in the straw. "Meh-eh-eh," she urged
them, pushing gently with her curved horns. The older black
and white one, struggled up onto its knees, wobbled, and
then collapsed. Moozeleh nudged it again. It bravely made its
way up, a tiny creature trembling on long, bony legs.

"I like that one," Elli said. "She's a brave one."

"She's a 'he,' a male kid," Mama corrected him.

Again and again, Moozeleh pushed the second kid, the
white one, bleating encouragement, until it also worked its
way up onto toothpick legs, blinked blearily around the kitchen and fell against its mother. She pushed gently again until the small white one was finally balanced.

Both kids butted and nudged uncertainly against her warm
sides until they found her teats and began to suckle. And
Moozeleh continued her work of licking and cleaning each
baby while they drank their fill.

"Now," said Papa, "We'll have to clear a place for Moozeleh and her kids in the storage shed."

"Oh no." Rifka felt her heart stop. "Can't they stay in here
where it's warm?"

"Two housewives can't share the same kitchen," Mama
laughed. Moozeleh and I would always be getting in each
other's way. Don't worry, it's nearly Passover time. The cold-
est weather is over. They'll be fine sharing the shed with the
geese and the chickens."

And with Shayndel's package and book, Rifka thought uneasily.

Papa lit a candle and led the way out to the shed. The
flame flickered and bent in the cold draft that came between

the rough wall boards. Strings of onion and garlic swayed against the thatch-topped rafters. The chickens, with heads tucked down on their breasts, didn't budge from their roosts on the rafters, but the geese in the coop stirred restlessly. Papa knelt to look in on them.

"They're twice as big as when you got them," he said with admiration. "I think they'll be ready for market in a few weeks."

"Papa, what will happen to the little boy goat?" Elli asked.

"Just as with Rifka's geese," Papa said, "we'll raise him until late spring, when he'll be big enough to slaughter for meat. The town already has a billy goat. If there were two they would fight with each other."

"So?" Elli's lower lip jutted out stubbornly. "I always fight with Zev. Just last week, he gave me a bloody nose."

"Don't talk like a child, Elli," Papa said abruptly. "Human beings are not the same as goats. Now Rifka and I have work to do." He turned away and began to move the flour barrel.

Elli stared at the geese for a minute and then stamped back into the kitchen.

"Ay, ay," Papa sighed. "Growing up is hard. Now what can we do to make room for Moozeleh?"

To Rifka's relief, he made no move to shift the pile of firewood. Instead they worked together and pushed the large barrel closer to the wall and moved full sacks against it. Soon they had made a cosy, protected corner which they piled high with sweet-smelling straw for bedding. Then Mama led Moozeleh out to the shed, Papa carefully carried each small kid out and placed it beside her and Rifka brought in a bowl of warm milk for Moozeleh.

Elli sat on the flour barrel chewing his lip, watching the kids suckle, getting angrier and angrier. When they finished and nestled in the hay beside their mother and fell asleep, he stormed into the kitchen to battle for justice.

"It's not fair!" he burst out.

Rifka stopped in the middle of memorizing "yoshavti, yoshavta, yoshavt..." Papa pushed his glasses up on his forehead, refocussing from a complicated problem in his Talmud, and Mama dropped a whole line of darning.

Elli clenched his fists, challenging Papa as he repeated, "It's just not fair. Boy goats must have a right to live, too. Otherwise why did God make them?"

Papa slowly removed his glasses and wiped them. "Elli," he said, "the Torah tells us that the fish of the sea, the birds of the air, the animals and the plants and trees were all given to man to use for his own needs. And we need male goats for meat."

Elli glared at Papa wordlessly. He couldn't argue with the awesome, age-old word of the Bible, nor could he argue with his father, but he couldn't accept their death sentence on the black-and-white kid, either. He gulped down a sob and stamped off to bed.

But Rifka could argue with anybody. Before Papa could get his head back into the Talmud, she was at him with her own question.

"Papa, maybe it *is* right for people to eat animals and to have animals like horses and oxen work for them. But do you think it's right for people to use other people as if they were horses and oxen, and make them work, and not pay them enough money to live on?"

Papa blinked at this new attack and peered over his glasses

at Mama. But she was deeply involved in the toe of Elli's sock, bending over to hide a smile.

"Why should old Lazer the water carrier work hard for other people all day, and not even have a pair of shoes to wear, when the Baron has an automobile and owns all the land around here, and I never see him doing any work at all."

"We can't expect perfect justice here on earth my child," Papa said. "This life is only a corridor, a dark, crowded hallway that leads to the wonderful, just world of paradise."

"Why can't we make it better here, now?"

"We try. Our Jewish law commands us to care for the orphan and the widow, to welcome the stranger, to give charity..."

"But Papa, why should there have to be poor people? My book says each person should do as much as he can for his town and his neighbors — and then each person should get back as much as he needs. That way nobody would be rich and nobody would be poor."

Papa smiled. "That will happen only after the Messiah comes. Nobody is that good. Our wise men gave us a more realistic law which tells us to take care of our own needs, but at the same time not to forget about helping others. 'If I am not for myself, who will be for me — but if I am for myself alone, what good am I?' "

"But..." Rifka began.

Papa pushed his glasses firmly into place and bent over his book, shutting her out.

Rifka lit a candle and went out to look at the goats. All three were warmly nested in the straw. The little ones were curled against each other, their heads on Moozeleh's soft, shaggy side, and she had curled her legs and head in a pro-tective circle around them.

Without reading Shayndel's book, Moozeleh had given as much as she was able to give that day, so even though she was a goat, she was entitled to everything she might need. Rifka quietly untied the sack of potatoes, put two in the empty milk bowl next to the goat's head and tiptoed out.

SEVEN

Goose Day

Goose day had come.

Rifka dunked and dunked and chewed and chewed but she couldn't swallow her black bread and cheese. As soon as she was done eating she'd have to go out and face her geese and do what had to be done. It was too hard to think about so she twirled the crust of bread unhappily, making whirlpools in the glass of milk.

Hooves clattered on the front porch. "Meh-eh!" Moozeleh's voice called as her head thumped at the door.

"Eh-eh-eh..." the shrill soprano of the two kids joined in.

"Pigs!" Mama scolded from the stove, "Wait a minute for your breakfast; you'll break the house down."

"Don't call the boy goat a pig, Mama," Elli said, "Zev and I gave him a name — Samson — because he's so strong, like Samson in the Bible."

There was more clattering, scratching and scrambling from the porch and suddenly a new, hollow thumping... this time on the roof. Bits of straw floated down past the kitchen window.

Mama, Rifka and Elli raced to the door and flung it open. Hungry Moozeleh scooted past them into the kitchen. At one end of the porch Papa had left a barrel that he intended to use for pickling beets for Passover, and on top of this barrel the little female kid teetered. She was reaching high up the wall with her forelegs, almost touching noses with her knock-kneed brother who was peering down from the roof.

"M-m-meh!" he urged her on and backed away from the edge tossing his head. His sharp little hooves thumped on the straw thatch as he explored this new playground.

"He'll eat up the roof," Rifka cried.

"Off, off, you good for nothing!" Mama yelled, "He'll ruin the roof and the rain will come in. If I get my hands on that goat I'll..."

"Don't get mad. He's only playing," Elli wailed. "He's just a baby."

"Rifka, get the ladder from the shed," Mama ordered, then ran in for the broom and found Moozeleh breakfasting blissfully on the beets in her shopping basket. With a furious swish of the broom, she sent Moozeleh out the door and off the porch. The small white kid tumbled over her own legs to follow her mother, as her brother wandered around on the roof.

Rifka and the ladder came bumping out of the shed. Elli helped her prop it against the wall. Before she could tuck up her skirt or even argue, he had scrambled up the ladder and crawled onto the roof.

"Hey, you, Samson!" he clapped his hands at the little goat who backed his way up to the roof ridge with his head lowered, ready to play war.

"Get down!" Elli whispered loudly. "Hurry up! Mama is mad. Aren't you in enough trouble already just because you're a boy?"

The kid's silly ears wobbled as he shook his head, stamped a black hoof and ducked around the chimney.

"Not here. We can't play here," Elli pleaded, "get down."
He crept forward.

The kid's eyes twinkled; he loved being chased. Waggling
his white flag of a tail, he scampered down the shed roof,
jumped to the fence and then to the muddy street below
where Moozeleh and the other kid waited.

"Phew!" Elli sighed. Then for the first time he realized
where he was — flat on his stomach on the steep slope of a
creaking, ancient straw roof, high in the air above everybody
else in the town of Savran. He raised himself shakily till he
was sitting up. The roof groaned dangerously as he moved.
Straw and tin rooftops and clay-smeared chimneys surrounded him. He could look right into Reb Leib's second-story
window. He saw the gleaming onion-shaped domes of
Savran's church rising beyond the marketplace. The muddy
Savrankeh River sparkled through the trees, swirling with
melted snow. On the far side of the river, the forest where
Papa cut wood was waking up with hints of the gray-greens,
yellows, and reds of springtime.

Very pretty up here, thought Elli. Then he thought
again... and froze with fear.

"Elli, get down here this minute!" Mama's voice floated up
from far, far away.

"I c-c-can't," he whispered.

"You'll catch cold, heaven forbid, and you'll be late for
school."

The morning breeze nipped under his shirt and through his
long underwear, and Elli's teeth began to chatter. Oh, how
he wished he were sitting at Reb Mendl's scratched wooden
table right this minute!

Rifka's head appeared at the roof's edge. "Elli, don't be

scared," she called, "just move to the edge by the ladder and I'll help you."

He stretched a leg backward, then yelped and grabbed for the chimney as the straw gave way beneath him and one knee sank through. And there he hung refusing to budge while Mama, Rifka, Aunt Miriam, Berelleh, the goats and the chickens shrieked advice and encouragement.

If Shloimeh the carpenter hadn't come past carrying a new table to Reb Leib's house, Elli might have spent the whole Passover holiday on the roof. Shloimeh quickly dragged over a second ladder, climbed up the first one, flung the new one across the roof till it rested on the ridge, then climbed it, plucked Elli up, flung him over his shoulder and carried him down.

"This is the way people are rescued who fall through the ice," he explained. "Remember children, you may need to know this next winter."

"Ice, shmice," said Mama, "the first thing to know is not to keep little male goats. I'll fix him, that mischief!" She shook her finger at the fleecy kids playing tag around and around Berelleh.

"Today of all days, right before Passover, the day we're taking the geese to be sold, today the goat chooses to climb the chimney."

"Just the roof," Elli sniffed.

The worst part of Elli's day was over, but for Rifka it was just starting. She dreaded going into the shed and facing the trusting eyes of her geese. You love goose fat smeared on Sabbath bread, and you like a warm goose down quilt, she argued with herself, and you need books to pass your exam, right? Right. Well then, get to it.

She clenched her fists and marched in.

The chickens huddled on the rafters and watched as white feathers flew in all directions and the shed filled with hissing and flapping. One by one, the protesting geese were pulled out of their crate and their legs tied together. Even the kids stopped playing and crowded the doorway to watch with wide, astonished eyes.

At last, Rifka was done; the trussed-up geese lay quiet and limp. Rifka's hands, arms, and ankles ached with nips from the yellow bills and without daring to take a minute to think or to mope, she and Mama loaded them into a borrowed

pushcart and trundled them off through the rutted streets toward the marketplace.

"Wait for me, I'll help you sell!" Raizelleh flew down her steps and caught up with them.

Rifka sniffed and looked away.

"What's the matter?" Raizelleh asked. "You look like you're going to a funeral."

"Tch, tch, tch," Mama clucked and shook her head, "Raizelleh, you said exactly the wrong thing. Cheer up, little daughter. You worked hard to fatten these geese, and soon you'll have the money you need."

"I feel like a murderer," Rifka whispered.

"Well, just help me get to the marketplace," Mama said, "and I'll take care of selling the geese for you. You can go and see about your books."

"Easter herbs, incense herbs!"

"Ribbons and thread!"

"Fresh fish — lively, jumping fish!"

"Books for women and holy books for men!"

"Clay pots, clay mugs, clay jugs!"

The hubbub of voices rose in the fresh spring air and drifted over the busy street. Housewives bargained, peddlers sang out their merchandise, pigs squealed, and chickens squawked. Easter and Passover were both coming in two weeks, and it seemed as though all the people of Savran and of the farms nearby were either buying or selling for their holidays.

Raizelleh wanted to shop for ribbons, but Rifka dragged her down the middle of the street past Chayim's stand covered with bright fabrics, and past the well where chunky Fedka the constable sprawled on his stool. They squeezed between crates of watchful chickens and baskets of early onions until they reached the hand cart of Bentchik the bookseller.

"Did you bring the books Shayndel asked you for, Reb Bentchik?" Rifka asked excitedly. "I'll have the money today."

"What, what?" Bentchik pushed the glasses lower on his long, bumpy nose and tipped his head to hear. "Ah-hah, Reb Mosheh's Rifka. Tch, tch," he clucked and shook his head. "Why does such a pretty girl, almost old enough to get married, want books on Russian geography? If you *must* read I have some good stories, some novels, the women's Bible in Yiddish..." He shuffled through his merchandise.

A gawky boy with a fuzz of new reddish mustache looked up from the opposite side. "Do you want this?" He lifted a large book and opened it to show her a double-page map. Well *I* have it," he grinned teasingly.

"Leibel, that's mine," Rifka cried, "That's the geography book Shayndel asked for. And isn't that Europe you're holding up?" She ran around the cart to look more closely.

Raizelleh shrugged. This interest in maps made no sense at all. She looked at Rifka and Leibel leaning close together as they examined the map of Europe. Well, she reconsidered, maps might be a bore, but Leibel the baker's son was interesting. She licked her finger, curled her two front curls around it tightly and then went to look at the book over the boy's shoulder.

With a long forefinger, he was tracing the course of their own Boog River from far up in the Northern Ukraine, down through the fertile farm land near Savran, and out past Belta and Odessa to the Black Sea.

"Belta, that's where I'll go to take my exam for the high

school," Rifka said. "That's why I need this book to study..."

"Look here," Liebel interrupted, and his finger moved along the map, "if you just sail past Belta, through the Black Sea and into the Mediterranean you're just a few day's boat ride from the Land of Israel. Here it is, right here. And that's where I'm going just as soon as I get old enough."

"You mean the Land of Israel from the Bible, where King David and King Solomon lived?"

"That's it. The Holy Land."

"Is it still there?"

"Of course, lands can't disappear. But it's not a land of milk and honey anymore, it's all barren and rocky and it's waiting for us Jews to come back."

His eyes shone with excitement and Rifka noticed they were a beautiful color — a mixture of honey and chocolate.

"That's enough, children," Bentchik pulled the book away and shut it. "Keep your fingers out of the books. You get them dirty. Leibel, don't fill the girls' heads with nonsense. The Land of Israel is not ours, it's owned by the Sultan of Turkey. And until the Messiah comes down from heaven and leads all the Jews back — which may take a while yet — the Sultan will continue to own it.

"So, young ladies, how about a nice romantic story about a prince and a princess?"

Rifka flushed. "Reb Bentchik, I am *not* interested in romantic stories. Please hold the geography book while I go and get money from my mother."

"In the meantime," Raizelleh said, turning to Leibel with a dimpled smile, "would you tell me more about the Land of Israel?"

He was watching Rifka move quickly away through the crowd.

"Leibel?"

"Uh... oh yes."

EIGHT

Chayim's Easter Riot

Red Leb, the carrot head,
Red Leb, the carrot head.

Rifka hummed to herself as she skipped past the chicken crates and leaped over a fat sow sunning herself in the middle of the marketplace. The Land of Israel and Leibel with the honey-chocolate eyes, so much to think about. For no reason at all, Rifka found herself grinning a great, wide, happy grin.

A new table sparkling with colors caught her eye. Peasant women in bright print kerchiefs and wide skirts crowded around it. She peeked through to see dozens of Easter eggs dyed red or painted in rainbow patterns like a garden of bright flowers.

Ahead of her, a forest of silvery-green branches seemed to be walking up the street from the Savrankeh River. Rifka slowed down and stared — walking trees? Then she laughed as she realized they were tree limbs carried high by a group of boys. "For Palm Sunday!" she exclaimed, remembering what Fanya had told her about the holiday. So many interesting things in the world — such a fine, lovely world! She skipped higher and harder for sheer joy.

Suddenly, angry shouts tore through the hum of market sounds.

"No, I didn't steal it. I paid. Give it to me!"

"Thief! Put that down."

A red-faced peasant woman tugged fiercely at one end of a long strip of print material. Chayim the cloth merchant had a firm grip on the other end.

"You didn't pay a cent. Put it down and I'll forget about the whole thing."

"I bought it. I paid for it," she shrieked, her shawl falling to one side and her hair flying loose.

"Put it down. I'll give you a special cheap price. Stop screaming."

"I paid, I paid!" The women yelled even louder.

"What's happening?" People in the crowd called out. "She said she paid, leave her alone."

The forest of willow branches charged forward.

"Money-grabbers, bloodsuckers!" one of the boys yelled and swept his branches across the table, knocking bolts of cloth to the ground.

"Exploiters, robbers, stealing from a poor woman!" Two others began to rock the table.

"Oh no, no. He's not a robber," Rifka cried, pushing through the crowd, "He's a good man! He's my father's friend."

"Bloodsuckers!" Others took up the cry as the fabrics tangled and fell in a swirl of color.

Chayim's wife ran to push off the attackers while Chayim dropped the end of cloth and tried frantically to save the rest of his merchandise. The peasant woman stuffed the cloth up into her wide, embroidered sleeve and disappeared into the shouting, milling crowd just as Rifka reached the table.

"Stop it! He's a good man," Rifka pleaded, tugging at the shirt of a boy who was struggling to overturn the table. His

elbow slammed back into her jaw. "You stop that!" she yelled and began pounding his back and kicking his ankles. Suddenly, her fingers were wrenched loose, she was lifted, and carried backward. Rifka struggled and squirmed around to find herself staring into a strange but oddly familiar face; pale, deep-set eyes under thick blond hair, square high cheekbones and thin lips that were sternly ordering, "Be quiet!"

She froze.

When they reached the edge of the crowd, he dropped her like a sack of potatoes and was gone.

Fedka the constable ran past, ploughing through the people and bellowing, "Get back! Go on, go about your business! I'll put you all in jail, you peasant pigs!"

Muttering and shaking their fists, men and women began to move away. Fedka continued to shout, waving his arms at white-faced Chayim and his panting, shaken wife and at the few remaining bystanders. Slowly, the normal cries of buyers and sellers began to rise again.

Rifka picked herself up, but her knees wobbled like fish jelly, like the day she had gone ice skating. And suddenly, remembering that day, she knew the face. It belonged to the man with the package, Shayndel's young man.

She stumbled forward, tripped on a fallen willow branch and squeezed back tears of anger. Why did they do that? Why did they assume Chayim was the thief and not the woman? Why did they call him bad names? How could they wreck his merchandise and hit him?

Somebody's neat, black-buttoned shoes were keeping pace with her own. A quiet voice said, "Don't be angry. The peasants are really good people. They don't mean to hurt anybody. They're just ignorant and they don't know who their real enemies are."

Rifka looked up to see Shayndel walking beside her.

"We'll teach them," Shayndel said, his eyes bright with determination.

"And for heaven's sake, Rifkalleh, don't ever run into a mob like that again. You could've been killed if Sasha hadn't dragged you out."

"Sasha?"

"Comrade Sasha. You'll be seeing him again soon. We have big plans for next month. We're going to turn things upside down, and soon I'll be needing that package. Hush now."

"Mama had seen them coming and rushed forward. Her

face was as white as the feathers of the two remaining geese. She drew her daughter close and held her without a word. Then, after a long moment, she pushed Rifka away again and said briskly, "Well, you have six rubles clear profit from the sale of the geese. That should buy you enough books to graduate from the university!"

NINE

The Passover Bargain

The rain pounded on the roof, leaked through the straw thatch and dripped into Mama's wooden bread-kneading trough. Papa hadn't had time yet to fix the hole made by Elli's knee.

"Ah, if Velvl were here..." Mama sighed and bit her lip.

In Velvl's last letter, he had written that he had a job operating a sewing machine in a cap-making shop in New York City. He was earning eight dollars a week and hoped to get a second job for part of the night so he could earn more money. He missed the family and wished them a happy, peaceful Passover. Mama wiped her eyes with a corner of the tablecloth she was patching. How could the holiday be happy with her oldest child across the ocean and her grandchild in another town? As for peaceful... there was an uneasy undercurrent in town ever since the fight in the marketplace. There were still mutterings on market days... bloodsucker, exploiter. She smiled wryly — what rich exploiters we are. I'm sewing a new patch on top of an old patch on my very best tablecloth for the Passover Seder.

The drip-dropping into the trough slowed and Mama heard Rifka's voice softly memorizing Russian grammar.

That was another worry, Mama thought. Rifka was working so hard, hoping so much to pass her examination. But if she passed and was allowed to enter school, it would take her away from the life of the family and the town. If she failed, it would break her heart.

Just then, a blaze of sunlight burst through the misty window and splashed gold across the table and the open grammar book. Rifka blinked in the brightness and looked up. "Hurray!" she cried, "it's done raining. That's enough grammar." She shut her book. "Mama, I'm going out to hunt for the new eggs. You can use them for Passover sponge cake."

"Kish, kish, kish," Rifka flapped her apron and called to Broyneh, the chicken.

"Ssss, sss," Rifka's two-year-old cousin Berelleh puffed and hissed behind her.

The chicken squatted deeper down in the hollow between two pieces of firewood and glared with unblinking yellow eyes.

"Kish, Kish! move, please. Oh, come on, Broyneh, don't be selfish, you can always make another egg tomorrow.

"Kish...Kish!"

The apron whisked past Broyneh's yellow beak, stirring her wattles. Berelleh waved his grubby hands and set the strings of onions swinging. Slowly the chicken backed off, tucking her head between her shoulders. Then she scrambled to the top of the firewood and flapped from there to the ground, squawking and scolding.

Rifka dipped into the hollow and pulled out a smooth, warm, brown egg. "That makes seven," she counted, slipping it into her apron, "and Mama has nine more inside."

Berelleh, who was crawling around and hunting in the straw, began grunting and tugging. "What's dis?" he called.

Rifka spun around to see only his round rear sticking out from behind the firewood, as he struggled to pull out Shayndel's heavy sack-enclosed package.

"Leave it! Don't touch!" she shrieked.

He scuttled backward so quickly that he flipped over with his legs waving like a turtle's.

"Ow, aaah, maah!" he yelled.

"You're all right, Berelleh." She hastily kicked some straw over the package, lifted the little boy, and dusted him off. "Stop crying."

"What's dat? I want dat!"

"Oh, that's nothing. Come on, we'll get some bread and jam for you to eat. Then you can take dry bread and feed the goats." She half pulled, half carried him into the kitchen.

Rifka's next chore was to get a pail of lime at the grocer's for whitewashing the walls. She clattered down the drug store steps and found Shayndel alone. "Please take the package already. I'm afraid," she blurted, and told her what had just happened.

"Another few days," Shayndel reassured her. "We're meeting during Passover week. It will be gone by then, I promise."

As soon as Rifka had lugged home the heavy pail of lime, she and Mama began to pull out the furniture and scrub it down in the afternoon sun. This pre-Passover changeover would turn the house upside down and inside out. The stained walls and chipped dishes, the heavy black bread and bean stew of the workaday world would all be swept away, at least for a week, by the great holiday of freedom. Their food would be special and they would eat it on one-week-a-year Passover dishes.

Mama rolled up her sleeves and tucked her kerchief behind

her ears and they sang together as they scrubbed. Little Berelleh kept time banging on the fence while he shared bites of bread with the black-and-white kid.

"You have a whole orchestra here," Papa laughed, and swung Berelleh high in the air. He had come home early to fix the roof before it got dark. "There are only three more days left. If I don't get it done now, it will have to wait till after the holiday."

"And if it rains," Mama said, "our whole Seder table will float away. We'll celebrate like Noah in the ark."

Every day after that was a breathless race to prepare for the great spring holiday of freedom. The walls were whitewashed inside and out and the closets and shelves were emptied and freshly lined. Papa hurried home early to strain his raisin wine. Later, he went to the public bathhouse to bathe before baking matzah. Then he and Elli took the Passover flour to the special bakery where they mixed, kneaded, and baked flat round loaves of matzah which would be used during the holiday instead of bread.

The sun and the trees and the busy breeze all worked together to dry the puddles, to coax the leaf buds to uncurl, and to put a wiggle of spring excitement into the waddle of the ducks and the jumping and wrestling of the children. Moozeleh's two kids butted each other and played hide-and-seek with Berelleh and Meyer in front of the house, while Aunt Miriam kept up an enthusiastic stream of spanking, scolding, sweeping, and scrubbing that could be heard halfway to Belta.

Rifka stuck her soapy fingers in her ears. "Aunt Miriam

prepares for Passover as much with her mouth as with her hands!"

The day before the holiday, the little house sparkled with newness, newly whitewashed walls, new gold sand on the floor with a handsome border stripe of red clay, and a newly-mended straw roof.

At dusk, Papa lit a candle and took a large wooden spoon and a feather. With Rifka and Elli's help, he poked into every corner, sweeping stray crumbs of bread into the spoon. Mama smiled and watched, her hands folded over her white apron, until Papa announced, "We have inspected the house and it is clean of every bit of *hometz*, non-Passover food. The house is ready for Passover!"

Early next morning, the thump of the chopping knife woke Elli and Rifka. Soon the hot, peppery steam of gefilte fish drifted from the kitchen. A little while later, there was the fragrance of dumplings dunked in onion and chicken fat, then soup, chicken, potato pudding, sponge cake.... The cloud of cooking smells rising from the whitewashed kitchens of Savran that day could make all the angels in heaven drool. Rifka snatched a matzah meal pancake to keep herself going.

"Nearly finished," Mama said in midafternoon. "Check the Seder plate, Rifkalleh. You should know what to put on it; after all, you'll be a housewife one day — unless you become a prime minister or a professor first." Her eyes twinkled.

"That's not so funny. Maybe I will," Rifka said huffily. "Let's see, a roasted lamb bone and a roasted egg to remember the sacrifice at the Temple in Jerusalem. Bitter herbs — yech — to remind us how bitter it was to be slaves in

Egypt. Haroses, the apples and nuts mixture — yummy —
for the mortar used between the bricks the slaves made for
Pharoah. And parsley for the greenness of springtime!
Right?"

"Right. Put the plate on the table next to the matzah and
then we'll get washed and dressed. Tonight I'll be a queen
and you'll be a princess."

At twilight, Mama lit the holiday candles. Men and boys
came home from the synagogue calling to each other,
"Happy holiday."

Little Berelleh and little Meyer sat at the table under
Aunt Miriam's stern eye. Uncle Ephraim, looking very
modern in his white paper collar, and Papa, in a white robe,
leaned back on their royal pillows. The two queens, the prin-
ces, and Princess Rifka waited eagerly for the retelling of the
ancient story of the Jewish people's liberation from slavery.

Papa rose, opened the Haggadah, the book which tells the
Passover story, and recited the blessing over the wine.

After a bit more reading, he broke a matzah into three
pieces and carefully tucked the middle piece, the Afikomen,
between his pillows. "This Afikomen is our dessert" he announced. "Without it, we can't finish the Seder. Now, who
will ask the Four Questions?"

Elli jumped up eagerly and, with Berelleh piping in a word
from time to time, asked, "Why is this night different from
all other nights...?"

The kings and queens took over, singing together the
stories and songs of the Haggadah that began with, "Once we
were slaves to Pharoah in Egypt...." and went on to describe
the struggle for freedom and the great power of God who had
saved the Jewish people.

Berelleh fidgeted and kicked the table. Meyer sucked his thumb until his eyes blurred and his head plunked down into his dish. Rifka's thoughts wandered. Freedom... freedom... Velvl went to America to look for freedom, and Shayndel thinks a constitution will bring freedom, and Leibel is sure that only a Jewish homeland will make him free, and I — I just know one thing — I have to pass my exam.

Elli slipped from his seat, tiptoed past the adult's chairs and stole his hand between the big white pillows that formed his father's throne. Papa continued singing. Elli crept noiselessly back to his place with the Afikomen matzah tucked under his jacket.

At last it was time to eat. Mama hurried in and out, rosy with pleasure at the compliments to her cooking. Her back arched and her hands were red from work, but she knew that no ordinary, everyday, non-cooking queen like the Queen of England would receive such compliments.

When the feast was over, Papa smacked his hand on the table and called out, "Well, children, it's time to give everybody a piece of Afikomen so we can finish the meal and continue the Seder." He reached back and felt around between the pillows and then looked up with make-believe astonishment.

"I don't know what could have happened. It's not where I put it. Ay, ay, ay — some thief must have stolen it. Chaykeh," he turned to Mama, "has Moozeleh been in the house tonight?"

"We can't blame everything on Moozeleh," she chided him. "Maybe there are two-legged thieves here."

"Tch, tch, tch." Papa pushed his glasses up on his forehead and looked around the table frowning ferociously. When he

reached red-faced Elli, the little boy burst out laughing and said, "It was me. I stole it, and you never even noticed."

"Congratulations. You're an expert," said Papa. "But now I must have the Afikomen back so that we can finish the Seder."

Elli shook his head so hard that his earlocks bounced against his flushed cheeks.

"Name your price," Papa pleaded, "otherwise we'll have to sit all night."

The boy took a quick breath, looked across at Rifka for help and then exclaimed, "I want the little boy goat!"

Nobody spoke for a moment.

Then all the grownups seemed to burst out scolding and arguing at the same time.

"Well that's silliest... what's the matter with you?" Aunt Miriam shrilled, "Can't you ask for a new shirt or a knife or some chocolate like a normal boy!"

"Elli, that's not a fair request," Papa protested. "The kid has no purpose except to be butchered. He'll never give milk and he'll eat us out of house and home. Now be a good boy and ask for something else."

"He'll ruin the roof again. Don't be a child," Mama scolded.

Uncle Ephraim added a general background noise, blinking with astonishment and murmuring, "Well, well. Well!"

Elli got redder and redder, his lower lip stuck out stubbornly, his eyes were watery, and he just kept shaking his head from side to side.

"Me, too, I like the little goat," Berelleh piped up, then hushed as Aunt Miriam raised a broad hand.

"It *is* a holiday of freedom," Rifka said thoughtfully. "Elli is only asking that Samson should be free to live."

"Aha — another attorney for the defense," Mama groaned.

"A dumb animal does not understand freedom," Papa stated.

"Oh, Papa, you should watch him gallop down the street pushing a barrel, or playing tag with Elli in the meadow beside the clay pit. He's so happy he's almost laughing out loud. And then he looks so sad when we close the shed door at night. He must know about freedom."

"That's enough talk. We must finish this Seder." Papa said firmly. "Elli, this is my final offer. We'll keep the male kid until the fall, until the holiday of Sukkos is over. Maybe by then something will have happened to the town billy goat — who can tell?"

Elli sagged. This was Papa's "I've had enough" voice. He pulled the Afikomen from under his jacket and handed it across the table.

The wine cups were filled, the adults began to sing again, and after a while Elli and Rifka joined in. When the candles were burned down to stubs, they reached the final, best-loved Seder song — "Had Gadyo," "One Only Kid."

Elli smiled happily across at Rifka as they sang in a wailing singsong about a small goat, bought by Father for two zuzzim, which was eaten by a cat, who was bitten by a dog, who was beaten by a stick... and on and on... until final justice was handed down by the Holy One, Himself.

In the shed, the small male kid flicked a fly from his ear and snuggled more tightly against his mother and his sister.

TEN

The Dangerous Delivery

"Rifkalleh, come out and take a walk, and look at my new dress," Raizelleh called from the street.

"Right away." Rifka swept the left over bits of matzah into her apron pocket for Moozeleh and took a quick look at her reflection in the glass door of Papa's bookcase. Curly hair caught back in a pink ribbon, pink ruffled collar framing her stubborn, pointy chin, and a pretty white shawl which hid the too-high waist and too-short sleeves of her dress-up dress. She decided she looked just fine, made a face at herself, and hurried out.

"Look, look, look!" Raizelleh spun around. Her blond curls flew and her blue skirt floated up like an umbrella.

"Look at me!"

"Me, too!"

Tova and Sarah spun around with their sister.

"Haskel the tailor said everybody is wearing sailor dresses in St. Petersburg and Odessa — and I'll bet even in America," Raizelleh announced.

"Well, I'll be sure to ask Velvl in my next letter," Rifka answered sarcastically, feeling dowdy and very jealous. She pulled her shawl closer.

"See the bow in front? It ties and unties. And Haskel said there's half a yard of material in the collar alone," Raizelleh went on happily until she noticed Rifka's glum face.

88

"Rifkalleh, what's the matter? Oh, don't be mad at me because I have a new dress. I'm just lucky because I have two younger sisters. See — Tova is wearing the dress I wore at Velvl's wedding and Sarah is wearing the dress I got for my cousin Shmulka's circumcision. You're lucky, too, you don't have to fight with two pesky little brats and wash their hair and wipe their noses..."

"Stop apologizing, it doesn't bother me," Rifka muttered, "Dresses aren't important anyhow."

The streets were unusually quiet on this second day of the holiday. No peddler's pushcarts clattered to the market and no housewives dumped wash water in the streets. Even Lazer had put away his harness and heavy pails. This morning, he sat in the synagogue wearing his old black holiday coat — still toothless and poor, but a king for two whole days.

"I love Passover. No more coats, no more scarves." Raizelleh threw out her arms, grabbed Rifka's hand, and began skipping, raising the dust on the street. They bounced and flew, tugging each other and forgetting their freshly waxed shoes and white stockings in the joy of spring. The little sisters shrieked and galloped after them.

Somehow, Raizelleh had led the way to the silent, shuttered bakery, closed for the whole week of Passover when it was forbidden to eat bread made with yeast. Coming down the street toward them were red-haired Leibel, his father, and his older brother, Dov. They were just returning from morning prayers.

"A good holiday to you," said Leibel, his ears turning red. "Where are you walking to?"

"Just walking, maybe down to the river," Raizelleh answered.

"Go, go and walk, too," the baker said gruffly, poking

Leibel in the back. "A little fun on a holiday is a good thing. It'll keep your nose out of sinful books."

The older girls turned to walk to the Savrankeh and Leibel kept pace, kicking pebbles in a straight line. The little sisters fell back, giggling and whispering.

Tova burst out giggling, "I know who Raizelleh likes!"

Raizelleh kept walking as though she hadn't heard anything.

"Who, who?" Sarah called.

Raizelleh turned and shook her fist.

The little ones shrank back a few steps and then sang out, "Red Leb, the carrot head, Red Leb, the carrot head."

"Ooooh! I'll beat you all black and blue!" Raizelleh screeched and charged after them as they scattered like chickens.

Rifka smothered her giggles. Raizelleh was really paying for her new dress!

"That's dumb, to make fun of your hair and your name," Rifka said to Leibel.

"I don't care. Leibel isn't my real name."

"It is, too."

"No, it isn't. Leibel means lion, and since I'm going to be a free Jew in the Land of Israel, I'm going to change my name to the Hebrew word for lion — 'Ari.' Doesn't that sound better?"

She nodded.

"Then say it."

"Say what?"

"Ah-ree."

"Ah-ree," she mumbled, embarrassed.

"You're the first one I told," he said, and his ears turned red again.

"Even before your mother or your brother?"

"They wouldn't understand. They don't understand why I want to go to Israel. My mother just wants me to study and help Papa in the bakery and get married. And my brother... he's another story. Let's not talk about him."

They were walking down the sloping path to the river. The voices of women chatting while they pounded their wash floated up through the trees. Easter had ended and the Christian women were back at work.

"You know," Rifka confided, "my mother wants the same thing, just to get me married."

They looked sideways at each other and burst out laughing.

Fanya peered up from the large flat rock where she had spread the family's long winter underwear. "Finally got a boyfriend, Rifka?" she called. "I'll show you how to make a specially painted egg for him. That's what our girls give their best boyfriends at Easter time."

"He's not a boyfriend — we're just talking!" Rifka said indignantly.

"Just talking — ha!" Fanya cackled, as Rifka and Leibel escaped back up the bank.

Raizelleh met them halfway. "I have a message for you, Rifka," she called. "Shayndel wants you to meet her near the drug store right now."

"I'll walk you if you want," Leibel offered quickly.

"No you can't," Raizelleh said smugly. "She said she needs to see Rifka *alone*."

Shayndel was waiting outside the store, turning the pages of a Russian textbook. "Good holiday, Rifka. I forgot to give you the homework for our next lesson."

Rifka stared at her blankly. Her homework was neatly listed in the big notebook she had sewn together. How could Shayndel have forgotten?

"Just lean down here and take a close look at the book; here's what I want you to do."

As their heads drew close over the book, Shayndel murmured, "Somebody is watching so just nod at everything I tell you."

Her finger moved along the page and she said softly, "I must have the package tonight but I can't get it from you — I'm being watched." Then, as a door creaked open behind her, she said more loudly, "Now I want you to copy this whole page, and be careful with your handwriting. They're very fussy about handwriting at the examination."

Berl the clock fixer came up the steps and stopped beside them to wind his big pocket watch. "What, school work on a holiday?" he asked with surprise.

"Oh no, Reb Berl." Shayndel smiled sweetly. "We're just going over Rifka's work for the next lesson."

"She's a hard worker that one, a man's head on her shoulders." He shook his head, finished winding, and went down the street.

Shayndel looked after him, frowning. "How many clocks can there be to fix in Savran? Why is he still here, always snooping? That man worries me."

She turned to Rifka again.

"Help me. Not just for me, but for all of us, for freedom. Please bring the package to the bakery tonight. Knock three hard knocks and then three soft knocks. Nobody will suspect you."

"It's very heavy," Rifka wavered.

"Raizelleh will help. She'll do anything you ask, but don't tell her more than you must." Her voice grew loud again. "Also Rifka, I want you to list all the major rivers in Russia and the provinces through which they flow."

"Happy holiday to you." Two women strolled by.

"The same to you," Shayndel replied and turned back to her pupil.

"All right, I'll do my homework." Rifka said slowly.

A mouse scrambled around Rifka's shoe. She jumped back and smacked her head against the ladder.

"Owooo," she whimpered and quickly covered her mouth. What a brave revolutionary, she scolded herself, afraid of mice, afraid of the dark. She reached between the shed wall and the pile of firewood, felt the hard square outline of the package, dug into the sack covering, with her fingernails and pulled.

"Keraa..a," a chicken clucked sleepily from the rafters.

Thank heavens, the goats were asleep in the yard. Slowly, she inched the heavy package along the floor to an opening where a few of the ancient wall boards had crumbled. She pushed it halfway out of the shed.

"I'm going over to Raizelleh's, Mama," she announced back in the lamplit kitchen.

"So late? What for?"

"She promised to show me an embroidery stitch and... and maybe, we'll take a short walk."

Mama beamed at her. "Well, I'm glad you're finally interested in learning something practical. Take your shawl; it's still chilly in the evening."

The edge of the sack was invisible behind the soft, new

tufts of grass beside the shed. She looked quickly up and down the street. The windows of the small houses shone faintly under the bushy eyebrows of their straw roofs. Nobody was in sight. Gently, she eased the sack out. Straining and panting, she hoisted it over her shoulder and started toward Raizelleh's house.

A door flew open and two small boys ran across her path, nearly knocking her over.

"Hey!" she began to scold and then quickly bit her lip. Be quiet, don't attract attention, she thought and tried to stop shivering. Would the police put a twelve-year-old girl in jail, she wondered, and shivered again.

Raizelleh was waiting in the shadows beside her house, clutching a wash basket. Her kerchief was pulled forward over her face.

"I thought you'd never get here. I'm so nervous I'm getting a stomach-ache. I couldn't even finish supper."

They lowered the package into the basket and covered it with a towel. Carrying it between them, they moved toward the marketplace.

"Rifka, why is this such a secret?" Raizelleh whispered, "What's it for?"

"To help people."

"What people?"

"The peasants."

"Oh."

Their feet scraped on the cobblestones of the market street. The locked shops and the empty stands stood lonely in the moonlight. A few wagons tipped toward the ground made long diagonal shadows.

"But I don't know any peasants," Raizelleh whispered

again, "Why should I go sneaking around at night, almost breaking my arm to help them?"

The wooden wall of the well was ahead of them and they jumped as a dark figure moved out from behind it.

"Strafstvoytyeh, good evening."

It was Fedka the constable, puffing on his pipe and enjoying the mild spring evening. His small eyes flicked over them suspiciously.

"Two such fine young housekeepers doing the wash at this hour?" he asked, puffing smoke from under his drooping mustache. "Leave some work for tomorrow."

Rifka was sweating. She wanted to drop everything and run, but instead she forced her shaking lips into a smile. "Strafstvoytyeh," she answered in her best Russian accent.

"S-s-s-strafstvoytyeh," Raizelleh stuttered and they walked stiffly on.

"W-w-why?" Raizelleh's whisper was shaky.

"Why what?"

"I know we're doing something against the law because *you're* scared too. Why should we maybe go to jail for some old peasants when we don't even know any?"

"It's for everybody — to make a better world for all humanity — Jews too. Now hush!"

They came to the dark front of the bakery.

"Let's rest for one second," Raizelleh groaned, "my arm is coming off."

In the silence as they stopped, they heard steps behind them, and looked back just in time to see a man's shadow dodge into a doorway.

Without a word, they snatched up the basket as easily as if it were piled with goose down and flew down the street past the bakery, turned up the next lane which twisted between tiny houses like a snake, scrambled under a fence and threw themselves behind a row of barrels. Their hearts were pounding and their breath came in quick, aching gasps. A baby cried in the house beside them and a woman's voice sang softly.

They waited.

A minute later, they heard heavy, running steps in the street, coming closer, just beyond the fence next to them, and then moving on past, thumping more and more softly, until the night was silent again.

"Now!" Rifka whispered. They stumbled out, hurried back to the bakery, and knocked three hard knocks, then three soft knocks. The door opened immediately and they thrust the basket inside.

In the moment it took to empty the basket, the girls glimpsed a circle of people sitting on the floor around a single dim candle: a head of bright, gold hair, Sasha, and next to him sat Shayndel, and there was the baker's older son, and perhaps ten or fifteen other young people.

"Go quickly." The basket was pushed out at them, they turned, and ran.

"Never, never, never, never again! Never!" Raizelleh was babbling, while trying to settle her stomach with tea and bread.

Rifka sat limply, giggling with relief.

She pulled herself upright and gulped down some of her tea. "Please explain that embroidery stitch, Raizelleh. I want to show it to Mama when I get home."

The girls were concentrating very hard on a tiny satin-stitch flower petal when Raizelleh's mother came into the kitchen. She stopped in the doorway, folded her hands over her generous belly, and smiled fondly.

"It's such a pleasure to see good children learning to be proper homemakers and housekeepers. With all the terrible things I hear about young people these days, this really does my heart good!"

ELEVEN

Constitution, Revolution, and Strike

One of Shayndel's pamphlets made its way back to Rifka's house with the help of Peter the woodcutter.

A few days after the meeting in the bakery, Peter was working with Papa deep in the forest beyond the Savrankeh River. They had just brought a great pine tree crashing down. They sat down on the trunk for a rest and a quick smoke.

"Moshka, tell me what's written here," Peter said, putting down his pipe and pulling a folded piece of paper out of his shirt.

Papa began to read, caught his breath, and tried to keep his face stiff and expressionless as he finished. "Where did you get this?" he asked.

"A young man — one of ours — and a young woman — one of yours — came to the house last night and talked to me. They said some funny things." His eyes crinkled up at the memory and he laughed out loud. "You would have laughed to hear them, Moshka. They said that I, Peter, should own the forest, not the Baron. And that I should own the fields I plant, not the Baron. And they even said, listen to this..." he slapped Rifka's father on the back, "they even said you aren't paying me enough for my work, and you're an ex, ex, explo... oh, the devil knows what they called you — not I!"

Papa forced a smile. "Young people are never satisfied. They always want to change things. The paper is just asking the Czar to give us more rights, a little more freedom."

"Rights, freedom — pteh!" Peter spat into the carpet of pine needles. "More bread, more vodka — that's what we need."

"For that we have to work." Papa stuffed the paper deep into his pocket and reached for his axe again.

As soon as he got home, without a word to anyone, he crumpled the paper into a ball and pushed it into the cooking fire. Then he retired into a corner with his Prayer Book. Swaying back and forth he felt his mind struggling away from the comfort of the Hebrew prayers. Exploitation, revolution, constitution — the words of the pamphlet rang in his head.

"Almighty God, keep this land at peace," he prayed, "because without peace, we Jews will be hunted down by both sides."

In that spring of 1905, Shayndel, Sasha, and their comrades stole through the Russian countryside talking to the peasants, arguing with workers in the factories and with soldiers at their barrack gates. Slowly, the ideas of "constitution," "revolution," and "general strike" began to bubble like yeast in the docile, doughy mass of the Russian people.

In far away St. Petersburg, the Czar and his ministers smelled the ferment. They were making secret plans of their own. They would fight the revolution with the oldest, best weapon they had — anti-Semitism.

The strike came to Savran with a can of snuff. Shloimeh the carpenter hurried into the drug store on a bright May morning, sorted a few coins from the nails in his pockets, and asked for a can of snuff.

Shayndel's uncle shook his head apologetically. "We're all out of snuff. I ordered some, but the trains went on strike and stopped running so they didn't send us any."

"Out of snuff? How can a person sit and study the Bible after a day's work without a wake-up pinch of snuff in his nose to clear his brain? How can you be out of snuff?"

"The trains..."

"The trains? What do you mean — the trains went on strike? How can trains strike?"

"No, no, the railroad workers went on strike. On the first of May they began a strike against the government. They refuse to run the trains. They say they want a constitution."

"Idiots!" cried Shloimeh the carpenter. "What's more important, a constitution or a full pouch of snuff?"

He charged up the steps and ran across the street to Yukel's house, where the tiny front room had been converted to a stationery shop. There he found no snuff, also no cigarette papers, and no chalk for marking his wood.

Reb Leib stalked in, thumping his cane. His gold watch chain trembled on his belly as he complained, "Can you imagine such an uncivilized town — no mail today, no newspapers! How can a person run a business in such a town? Disgusting! Yukel, let me have some snuff."

Yukel shook his head solemnly. "I'm afraid, Reb Leib, that this is bigger than Savran. Malka," he called to his wife in the back room, "watch the store. I'm going out to find out what's going on."

By the time Rifka got to the marketplace to buy soup greens, with Berelleh tagging along behind her, the street was filled with groups of people discussing the strike. The largest number were gathered around Hirsh. His overloaded wagon had rolled in from Belta a short while before, carrying goods that had been left there because of the strike.

"Another load like this," he joked loudly, "and my horses will go on strike, too."

He unloaded the merchandise for Savran and was in a great hurry to water the horses and deliver his goods to the next town. To Berelleh's squealing delight, Hirsh allowed him to hold the horses' reins while Rifka brought them water, and he answered eager questions about what was happening in the outside world.

Yes, the railroad workers were on strike, and so were the post office workers, and the dock workers at the port of Odessa, and the textile workers. Even the young tailor boys in the shops of Odessa and Belta were striking. As far as he knew, the whole world might be on strike. The streets were full of police, and there was talk that the Czar might call out his Cossacks with their sabres and their horses. Then there would really be trouble.

What were they striking for?

He lifted his cap and scratched underneath thoughtfully. He had heard that they were asking for a constitution with laws that would be the same for everybody, so that everybody would be able to vote and decide how to run the country.

"Ay, ay, ay...as if we haven't got enough trouble with one Czar running the country—now we'll have ten million Czars sitting on our backs," Chayim groaned.

"No, Reb Chayim. You're wrong!" Shayndel's clear voice rang out from the edge of the crowd. "Nobody will sit on our backs. We'll all be free when we have a constitution. Everybody will obey the same laws—Jews and Christians, nobles and peasants. We'll throw out the special taxes and special land laws that punish only the Jews. All the people of Russia will be brothers!"

Leibel's brother Dov pushed through the crowd and handed out leaflets.

"What's dat?" Berelleh dropped the reins to pick up a paper that had fallen.

Rifka began to read it to herself, just as Shayndel jumped onto the seat of Hirsh's wagon and shouted the words out to the stores and pushcarts and people of the marketplace.

To the people of Russia:
The great day has come.
The revolution is here.
We must fight for our freedom and our constitution.
We must all vote like freemen, and own land like free-
men.
We must be ready to die for these freedoms!

"All of you—Hirsh, Chayim, Mosheh, Hannah—you and I can be part of this wonderful revolution—or we can be smothered by the tyranny of the Czar!"

"That's enough!" Hirsh growled. His ruddy face turned gray with fear. He stepped up and swung the young woman down from the seat.

"I have merchandise to deliver. Clear out of the way!" he bellowed. Rifka snatched Berelleh back seconds before the wagon lurched forward to the crack of Hirsh's whip and rolled creaking down the market street, quickly building up speed.

Suddenly she heard the driver cry, "Whoaa!" as he pulled his horses off to the side and reined in fiercely, straining backward with his whole body.

Pounding like thunder, a group of horsemen came gallop-

ing up the narrow road toward the wagon and swept past it into the marketplace. In a whirl of dust, they circled the well and pulled up, horses rearing and clattering, sending goats, chickens, and women with buckets running.

"Cossacks."

The dreaded name of the Czar's shock troops hissed through the marketplace.

Rifka pulled Berelleh tight against herself and tried to disappear behind Chayim's table of yard goods. She managed to peek through a space between the red-checked gingham and the blue velvet.

The riders waited, erect and rigid as statues. Their wickedly-curving sabres swayed with the movement of the horses. Rifka shivered. From the tall, fur hats and sweeping mustaches down to the flowing manes and stamping hooves, the Cossacks looked like huge, frightening horse-man monsters to her.

Fedka the constable came running out of the tavern at the end of the street, brushing crumbs from his mustache and buttoning his jacket as he ran. He puffed up to the lead horseman, bowed respectfully, and exchanged a few words. Then, as swiftly as they had come, the horsemen whirled, swept out of the marketplace, and disappeared down the road to Belta.

"They're going to smash heads someplace, those blood-thirsty beasts. Thank heavens it won't be in Savran," Chayim murmured grimly. "It's lucky for Shayndel that Fedka didn't hear her wild talk about a constitution."

He pushed Rifka gently. "Better go home, Rifkalleh. There may be trouble here yet."

She looked around for Shayndel, but there was no sign of her.

"Come on, Berelleh." She yanked him along. "Let's get the soup greens and go home."

At that moment, all Rifka wanted was to be sitting, safe and hidden, on the floor beside the heating wall or on the straw in the shed, with a kid nestled against her. How could Shayndel be so brave?

"I'm tired," Berelleh complained.

"We're almost home," Rifka said and took a short cut through the alley beside the tavern. At the far end, two men stood in close conversation. She recognized Fedka's broad shoulders and thick neck. The other, smaller man, with his face turned away might be Berl, Rifka thought. Why would he be here with Fedka? The men disappeared into the back door of the tavern before Rifka and Berelleh could reach them.

That evening, Papa came heavily up the steps, put his axe beside the door, and leaned against the doorway.

"Mosheh, what the matter. Are you sick?"

"No, I'm fine. But there's news."

"We know." Rifka and Elli looked up eagerly. "There's a strike and the Cossacks came through."

"No, not just news — bad news."

Mama's mending dropped into her lap.

"Fedka and his police arrested Shayndel, Dov, and three of Haskel's tailor boys, and took them off to jail in Belta for inciting to revolution."

"Aaah," Mama began to rock back and forth on the bench sighing softly. "Ah, the crazy young people. Why, why do they do it?"

TWELVE

The Happy-Sad Spring

Kvetcher the rooster stretched his neck and crowed up into the blue dawn. The goats thumped against the shed wall, turned over, and tucked their noses under their legs again. Scatterbrained chickens might be up and about, but it was much too early for goats. Water splashed into the basin as Mama washed and set potatoes to cook for breakfast, and Papa's voice softly murmured the morning prayers.

Rifka opened her eyes a crack and then squeezed them shut. Morning was the worst time — it was her thinking, worrying time. Please, please, let it be a dream that Shayndel and the others are gone, she thought. When I open my eyes again let everything be the way it was before last week. Please.

Mama had kept her busy, and Aunt Miriam, who was complainingly pregnant again, often needed her help with the little boys, but still the days felt empty. Rifka's books lay piled on the shelf, untouched. She missed the quiet lessons at the dining room table, listening to Shayndel's soft, patient voice and laughing with her over a funny name or a silly mistake. She pushed back panicky thoughts of what might be happening to her teacher behind the gray stone walls of the Belta jail.

The thumping from the shed began again, as the light in the room brightened. Mama would be calling her to get up

106

and milk Moozeleh soon. She stretched just enough to jab Elli, asleep on the cot next to hers, and then escaped to the kitchen before he could jab back.

By milking time, in spite of herself, she felt happier. Sunlight poked between the boards of the shed wall and Moozeleh crunched contentedly on beet greens, potato peel, and bread crusts while Rifka squeezed the warm milk from her teats into the pail. The goat's udder was full from her rich springtime diet and gave a pitcher of foaming milk at each milking. Each week, there was enough leftover for Rifka and Elli to bring a cloth-covered pitcher of milk to Lazer the water carrier. Mama let the extra milk get sour and thick. Then she poured it into cloth sacks which hung from the ceiling to drip, until the water separated out and the creamy curds were ready to squeeze into cheese.

Such a good time, Rifka thought, too early for mosquitoes and other bugs, but just right for sun and poppies and violets and the first strawberries. But the worry for Shayndel kept popping up to overshadow the springtime joy.

Everyone had worries, even Elli.

They were picking berries one day when he asked, "Rifkalleh, why did Shayndel have to go and get Fedka mad by yelling about socialism?"

"Because she thinks it's good."

"Why?"

"Because it teaches everybody to share what they have."

"Like you and me sharing Velvl?"

"No, it's sharing *things*. If I had two cows I'd be glad to give you one. Or if I had four loaves of bread I'd give you two loaves. Or if I had two pairs of boots I'd give you one pair. Understand?"

"Sure, it's easy."

"All right then, you try it. If you had two cows, would you give me one?"

"Oh, yes."

"And if you had four herrings, would you give me two?"

"Sure."

"What if you won ten buttons in the button game, would you give me five?"

"No!" He shook his head vigorously.

"Why not?"

"Because I *have* ten buttons and I need them all. I don't mind sharing things I don't have, like cows or herrings, but I need my buttons."

"Oh Elli, you're so dumb!" and she dumped an armful of grass on his head.

That evening, Mama, Rifka, and Aunt Miriam sat together dipping into the sack of goose feathers, separating the soft down from the harder feathers to make a new quilt. Mama's hands moved so fast they blurred in the lamplight.

Suddenly, she sighed deeply and repeated Elli's question, "Why did she do it?"

"For the people!" Rifka blurted indignantly. "She did it to make a better world."

"Yes, yes, I know. The world sent her a letter and said, 'make a revolution for me'," Mama scoffed. "You're talking childish nonsense. Poor Shayndel, for such nonsense she may sit in jail for the rest of her life."

"What do you expect?" Aunt Miriam said. A girl of twenty without a husband. If she had a husband and a baby or two to worry about, instead of a high school diploma, you can be sure she wouldn't be yelling about a constitution. I blame it all on her uncle for not getting her married in time."

"Husbands, husbands, husbands — with strikes and revolutions and Cossacks all around us — all you can think about is husbands!" Rifka jumped up and sent the down floating in all directions.

"Rifka!" she heard her mother's angry tone. "Show more respect for your elders."

Rifka stamped out of the yard, spilling over with anger and sadness and the awful, quaking fear that maybe they were right. After all, Elli wasn't ready to share. Who was? Were the peasants ready? Were the shopkeepers ready? If nobody was ready, then Shayndel and the others were sitting in jail for nothing.

Even the hours she spent teaching me were for nothing, Rifka thought. How can I take the examination in September if she doesn't come back? Won't Aunt Miriam be pleased! She kicked furiously at a rock, stubbed her toe, and hopped up and down getting angrier at Aunt Miriam, at Mama, at the Czar... even at Shayndel.

The peaked roof of the old House of Study loomed ahead. Light showed dimly at the windows and the open door. It was late, she knew the men had all gone home by now, but she glanced in as she went by. The light of one candle barely lit a long wooden table with a bench on each side. A pale, wispy-bearded young man sat alone at the table, swaying slightly as he bent over a book, keeping his place in the dim light with his finger.

"All by himself," Rifka murmured to herself, "and the holy books are so difficult."

She stood silently watching until the night air began to chill her bare feet, and then she turned to go home.

Well, why not? The question danced in her head. I couldn't make socialism or a constitution happen, even if I wanted it more than anything, but I *can* try to get ready for that exam by myself. As Papa said — "if I am not for myself, who will be for me?"

She walked faster and faster, and then started to run. She would study alone, and skip what she didn't understand, and then come back to it and circle it and sniff at it like the dogs in the marketplace sniff at new things, and study again. She wouldn't give up, she'd work for herself and for Shayndel, too!

Something else happened that happy-sad spring that made Rifka tingle whenever she thought of it.

One afternoon, she carried a load of wash down to the Savrankeh with her Russian history book perched on top. After she scrubbed the aprons, shirts, and blouses on a large, flat rock, she rinsed them in still icy water, squeezed them, piled them in the basket, and sat on a log to study. The sun's rays slanted low over the river, baking her bare legs. She dunked her legs and wiggled her toes and read.

A pebble flew over her shoulder and plunked into the water beyond her foot. Then another. She looked back, ready to yell at Elli, but instead saw Leibel leaning against a tree a little way up the bank, wearing a cap powdered with flour, with a book under his arm.

"Want a cinnamon roll?" he asked.

She nodded.

He came and sat on the log beside her, pulling two rolls out of his pants pockets.

"I'm not at school anymore. I'm working in the bakery," he said.

"Oh?"

"When they arrested my brother, my father said he needed me to help in the bakery. I don't care. I had enough of Reb Mendl."

"What's happening with your brother?"

"My father went to Belta and bribed the prison warden and got to see Dov for a few minutes. He's thin and pale. He told Papa that they keep asking him questions. But nobody would say anything about when he'd get out. Mama walks around all day blowing her nose and wiping her eyes."

"Did he see Shayndel?"

"No, she was in a different part of the building."

They chewed their rolls in gloomy silence.

"And it's all for nothing," he said at last. "All that crying and worrying is for nothing. Now if *I* ever have to go to jail it'll be for a good reason, for my own people."

Rifka jumped to Shayndel's defense again.

"They do, too, have a good reason! They're fighting to get freedom for us and for the rest of the Russian people. That's a good reason."

"That's a stupid reason. If the Russian people ever get freedom, they won't share it with us. They'll give us a fist in the face, like they always do."

"How can you talk that way?" she cried. "Russia is ours as much as theirs. And Jews and non-Jews can work together— look how Sasha and Shayndel were working together."

"They'll never let it be ours. Only Israel is ours."

Rifka got up, brushed the crumbs from her skirt, and said stiffly, "Thank you very much for the roll."

"Oh, please sit," he grabbed her arm, "I don't want to argue with you. Look, look — I'll show you something, just sit."

He picked up a small rock and threw it so it skidded and

bounced along the surface of the river almost to the other side before it sank.

"Can you make it walk on water like that, Rifkalleh?"

She shook her head.

"Like this." He skidded another pebble along.

She shrugged, threw one, and it plunked and sank.

"I'll show you." He came close, moved her arm way out to the side and back, then swung it forward. Suddenly his face turned red below the flour-whitened cap. Rifka felt a hot tingle race from her fingertips to her toes.

"I'll d-do it myself," she stammered, turning her face away, all warm and embarrassed, and tried again. Her pebble bounced once and sank.

She tried again. This time it bounced twice.

"Hurray!" He threw his cap in the air.

They both threw and threw again, laughing together, until Leibel suddenly smacked his cheek. "Uh-oh, I told Papa I'd only be gone a little while. I left a whole batch of dough rising."

They hurried up the bank carrying the wash basket between them. At the top, before they went in opposite directions, he asked, "Will you do the wash the same time next week? I'll bring poppy seed rolls."

"I'll try," Rifka answered, her eyes shining. She sang out loud all the way home.

THIRTEEN

America the Golden

"Waaah... aaah...waaah...!"

Rifka huddled over her grammar book, reciting verbs at the top of her lungs to drown out the baby's crying.

Elli stuck his fingers in his ears and grumbled, "Yosselleh this and Yosselleh that; go rock Yosselleh, get him some water, wipe his chin... you'd think he was the Messiah just dropped down from heaven."

Velvl's wife and baby had come from Belta to spend the Shavuos holiday with Rifka's family. And, as Mama said, the house immediately began to run on wheels, circling around and around the five-month-old baby. When Yosselleh laughed and gurgled, everybody cooed and giggled and cackled. When Yosselleh cried, Fraydeh and Mama were close to tears, too.

Right now, Yosselleh's gums were hurting and he was letting everybody in the house and in the whole town of Savran know about it. Mama paced back and forth nervously beside Fraydeh, who was also pacing back and forth with the teething, drooling, wailing baby draped over her shoulder.

Aunt Miriam bustled in the door. "Such wonderful lungs, no evil eye!" she cried enthusiastically. "Tch, tch, you both look wrecked. Give him here. On babies I'm an expert."

Fraydeh gratefully handed the little one over.

"Get me a clean rag soaked in cold sugar water," she commanded, bouncing the baby up and down and smacking his bottom energetically.

Mama ran, and Fraydeh collapsed on the bench next to Rifka. "I don't know how I'll ever manage him by myself on the trip to America," she sighed. "Wouldn't it be wonderful if you could come with me?"

"He'll be much bigger by then," Rifka said.

"Not much, if God wills it." Fraydeh's face brightened. "Wait till you hear what Velvl wrote in his last letter. I'll read it when it gets a little quieter."

Elli pushed close. "I want to hear, too. Did he see any Indians? Did he find gold?"

Fraydeh laughed as she pulled a pack of letters tied with a ribbon out of her straw suitcase and began to look through them. "Elli, I think Velvl went to a different America than the one you're always talking about."

Little sucking noises had replaced the howls as Yosselleh clamped his gums down on the rag. Aunt Miriam settled at the table rocking the baby and everyone drew close to hear the news from America.

"Here's a good one," Fraydeh said, "it's about a roaring tunnel."

She began to read:

Today I found a new wonder in New York, a tunnel filled with trains. I went down many steps into an opening in the ground, like your father's cellar — but much bigger — and found myself in a tunnel that runs for miles and miles under the buildings of the city. Trains thunder through this tunnel roaring like wild animals, day and night, Sabbath and weekday.

"Shameful," Mama murmured, "even on the Sabbath."

Papa would not be able to earn a living as a seller of wood here. People don't cook over wood fires, they use gas which comes through a pipe. And they use gas for their lamps, too, instead of kerosene. Candles are lit only for the Sabbath. In some houses, water comes right out of the wall through a pipe and doesn't have to be brought up from the street. And in Uncle Pinyeh's house, there is a toilet, which is a seat over a bowl with a box of water hanging on the wall above it. You just pull a chain and water rushes down to flush the bowl clean.

"My, my, my... what a pleasure — right in the house!" Aunt Miriam marvelled.

On the Sabbath, I stroll through the streets and hear a hundred languages — Yiddish, Russian, Polish, Italian, Greek — even Chinese. It's like the tower of Babel. How could they build a city with so many different languages? There is a park here which is always filled with people. Young men and even young women stand on benches and boxes and make speeches about their bosses and the unions, they even talk about voting for the government. Everybody who is a citizen can vote. And after a few years, anyone can become a citizen.
The houses are tall and close together and crowded with people, without a tree or a bit of grass between them. Sometimes I get tired and feel like a slave chained to my work bench, but my head and my heart are drunk with freedom, as if it were Purim and Passover together, all in one day. I can't wait until you and Yosselleh are with me.

"And now listen to this everybody," Fraydeh looked up with shining eyes.

I have already bought a steamship ticket for you. I pay a dollar from my wages each week and I hope I'll have it all paid up in a few months.

"May it be God's will that you should be together soon," Mama said gravely and kissed her on the forehead.

Yosselleh stirred and whimpered and Fraydeh hurried to put the letters away. It was time to nurse the baby.

"I have to tell Zev about the tunnel," Elli said, racing out the door. "I'll be right back."

Rifka went out, too, and sat on the steps. The stars hung low and bright, with just a sliver of moon showing. Lush, damp smells of the waking earth, the deep "chug-a-rum" of frogs from the watery clay pit, sleepy calls of birds bedding down... everything filled her. She loved this town. How would it be to live in that great busy Babel of America?

Well, it would be free. There were no Cossacks in America, no pogroms, no quotas.

Fraydeh's voice drifted out, singing a lullabye.

Under my little one's cradle,
Stands a snowwhite kid.
The kid will go to market
And sell raisins and almonds.
My little one will study Torah
And become a great, learned man.

But in America, Rifka thought with a sudden pang, there wouldn't be any Leibel, either.

Moozeleh's coat was ghostlike in the twilight. She came and

nosed into Rifka's apron pocket. Rifka grabbed her horns; they pushed affectionately back and forth until Rifka gave up and emptied the pea pods she had saved in her pocket.

"Sorokah, Voronah, Meezelleh, Maizelleh, Kitz, Kitz, Kitz..."

Yoselleh gurgled and kicked his short fat legs as Rifka made circles in his palm, repeating, "Sorokah, Voronah, Meezelleh, Maizelleh," and then at "Kitz, Kitz, Kitz," she ran her finger tickling up his arm.

He pushed his fist at her again for more. She bounced him to her other knee and sang, "Sorokah, Voronah..." again.

Rifka, Raizelleh, Yosselleh, and Aunt Miriam's Berelleh were waiting in the yard the next morning for Fraydeh to finish making knishes so they could all go to pick greens and flowers for the Shavuos holiday. The house and the synagogue had to be green and fragrant for this holiday of first fruits.

"Now let me." Raizelleh took the baby and began the chant.

Berelleh watched with big, jealous eyes. "Me, too," he begged.

"It's just for babies, not for big boys," Raizelleh said.

"Oh." His round cheeks sagged.

Rifka suddenly felt sorry for the little boy who had always been a big brother, never a baby.

"This is for big boys," she laughed and picked him up and swung him in a great, flying circle, faster and faster, until he shrieked with delighted terror, "No more, no more!"

Fraydeh came out, her arms filled with baskets and clay jugs of water for the flowers. The equipment was divided up and the procession set off, with the two kids trotting along for company. When they reached the meadow near the clay pit, Fraydeh spread her shawl on the grass and set Yoselleh down. He struggled onto his hands and knees and rocked back and forth making satisfied, clucking noises while the goats wandered around him chomping at the young grass.

Everyone else was working, cutting flowering branches, picking poppies, buttercups, and tiny violets and setting them in the jugs.

Fraydeh sang as she worked. Her kerchief was pushed way back and her hair strayed loose across her cheeks. She didn't look at all like a proper housewife — and a mother besides. "Oh, I love this holiday!" she cried. "What a beautiful time God chose to give us the Ten Commandments. It's all sun and flowers and babies and kids and new chicks — everything is new!"

Fraydeh dropped the branches and seized Rifka, spinning her around and around in a waltz. "And soon I'll see Vel-vel, Vel-vel, Vel-vel," she sang exuberantly to the tune of the "Blue Danube" waltz.

Laughing and dipping and tumbling over her feet, Rifka tried to keep step in the sweeping circles of the dance. Then Fraydeh dropped her arm and swept to Raizelleh and swung her into the steps of the dance. Rifka took Berelleh's hands and circled with him, singing along loudly, "Soon I'll see Vel-vel, Vel-vel, Vel-vel."

Yosselleh stopped rocking. He fell over on his side and watched in drooling amazement.

A tall, gaunt young man trudged up the road through the meadow. He was wearing a heavy sheepskin jacket and a cap, even though the day was warm. He stopped to watch, too,

lowering the sack he carried to the ground and tipping back his cap to wipe his forehead and straw-colored hair.

Rifka saw him and lost her breath for singing. The green meadow blurred, she suddenly felt the pushing and smelled the smell of the pre-Easter crowd, felt the anger and the ache at the side of her jaw. She dropped Berelleh's hand and walked toward the silent, watching man.

"Strafstvoytyeh, Sasha," she said. "Do you have news of Shayndel?"

He forced his eyes away from Fraydeh, who had stopped dancing and was looking toward them.

"Strafstvoytyeh. We have heard that she is well."

"When…" Rifka began.

"Certain people are trying to help." he interrupted. A

quick smile flickered through his deep-set eyes, "I hope she'll be able to study with you soon."

He hoisted his pack up, pulled down his cap, and went on toward town.

Crusty, brown cheese-and-potato knishes were cooling on the table when they came in with their arms full of flowers and leafy branches.

Mama was mixing sour cream into the beet soup and humming over her work. "Such beautiful flowers!" she cried. "What a fine Shavuos feeling; you've brought the fields into the house. Girls, take most of the greens over to the synagogue. Fraydeh will put the rest around the house."

Rifka and Raizelleh hurried through the streets, anxious to finish and get back to the knishes. They clattered up the worn wooden steps and pushed open one of the tall, creaky doors. Solemn quiet billowed out at them. The synagogue was empty; everyone was at the bathhouse or at home preparing for the holiday.

Timidly, they moved down the center of the large room. Except for the freewheeling Simchas Torah holiday, they were never down here in the men's section, not since they'd been little girls sitting beside their fathers and playing with the silk fringes of the prayer shawl. Now that they were growing up, they always climbed the staircase beside the doorway and sat on the small, crowded women's balcony, hidden by a lattice from the sight of the men below.

The light was dim. The air smelled mustily of many years of people and books and prayers and tears. Here was Papa's seat, near the *bimah*, the reading platform in the center of the room. Velvl always used to sit right beside him. On the eastern wall of the wooden building, there was a splash of scarlet and gold — the *aron kodesh*, the closet of the scrolls of the Law, covered by a red velvet curtain. Above the closet, two fierce carved lions leaned toward each other, gleaming softly with gold leaf.

"Where do we put the flowers?" Raizelleh asked. "Hurry, they're making me sneeze."

"Let's put them on the reading platform."

"Up there? Us?"

"Sure. Nobody is praying. It's all right."

They climbed the steps, put their branches down and began to lace the greenery through the carved posts of the railing and then twined them up the four corner posts. The freshness of woods and fields crept into the still air. Pale purple and pink and sunny yellow sparkled against the somber wood in honor of the holiday of early summer.

Rifka finished. She ran her fingers over the carved leaves and flowers on the side of the reading table. This was where the parchment scroll of the Torah would be unrolled the next morning, and this was where Velvl had stood and read the Bible to the whole congregation before he was married. Did he miss this in golden America? Rifka wondered. She peered up to the women's balcony above with its seats hidden by the screen.

"Come on, Rifkalleh, we're finished. We shouldn't be up here." Raizelleh pulled her arm.

"Why not? It's our synagogue and our Bible as much as the men's."

"I don't understand you at all!" Raizelleh ran down the steps. "You make a fuss about such silly things. Some things are just for boys and some things are for girls. Why do you have to argue about everything? Well, I don't care, do what you want, *I'm* going."

Rifka laughed and ran to catch up with her friend. From the doorway, they turned to look back. The reading platform was like a tree house softly wrapped in green leaves and pastel flowers in the center of the dim, closed room.

They smiled at each other proudly and then turned and ran, to get back before Elli could finish the knishes.

FOURTEEN

Summer Worries

That summer of 1905 was a waiting time.

People scratched mosquito bites and pickled tomatoes and made clay bricks to dry in the sun — all the usual summer work — but they worked with one eye looking over their shoulders, holding their breaths a little bit, waiting. After all, how long can a pot plop and bubble and steam without boiling over?

That summer, in the port of Odessa, the crew of the largest warship in the Russian fleet — longer than Savran's main street — mutinied, killed their officers, turned their guns on the city, and bombarded it.

Strikes were breaking out like little flickers of fire, here and there, all over the country. For the time being, the trains were running again, but nobody knew for how long.

People were plucked off the street and dragged away to jail or to exile in the icy North just for mentioning the word "democracy." Fedka the constable got orders from the district police chief to hire six new policemen in case of trouble in their own town.

Elli and Rifka had waiting problems, too.

All day long, Rifka talked to herself, mumbling multiplication tables, verbs, names of rivers and cities. Moozeleh became the best-educated goat in Savran as she listened to Rifka during milking time. Studying, waiting for Shayndel to return, waiting for her exam in September... it was a long summer.

But for Elli, the summer was too short. He was waiting for something to happen to the town billy goat. The New Year holiday was coming closer and Samson's lease on life was running out. Each day on his way home from school, Elli checked hopefully, but the tough old male sprawled comfortably in the marketplace among the lady goats, flicking flies from his coat. When Samson trotted to meet him, butting him playfully, Elli had to gulp down worried tears.

In the evenings, Papa and Rifka shared the dining room table, both studying softly. Papa drank cup after cup of tea as he puzzled his way through the complicated arguments of the Talmud. How could one man absorb that much tea and that much Talmud without spilling over, Rifka wondered. Once, when the murmur of his voice stopped, she looked up to find him watching her with a strange look, a mixture of pride and anxiety.

"All learning can be good, Rifkalleh," he said, "and I'm proud that you are learning about the world around you. But you must remember that the only true learning is the learning that brings us closer to God and to our fellow man."

She turned back to her history book, puzzled. Did Papa mean he *was* glad she was studying, or he *wasn't?* Maybe a little of both. She shrugged, and plunged back into her work. Study had to be good, she was sure of it, it was her steamship ticket to the whole world, to the future.

One airless, hot evening, Papa's closeness to his fellow man was tested. Mama had just put the supper of herring and black bread on the table when they heard blood-curdling shrieks from the street. A minute later, the door flew upen and Fanya charged through and scrambled around the table to hide behind Mama. Her red-faced husband came crashing in, waving his fists and bellowing, "Give her to me! I'm going to kill her!"

Papa sprang up, grabbed Peter's shoulders and wrestled him back toward the door, shouting, "Peter, no! Leave her be. Whatever she did, leave her be."

"I'm going to kill her!" Peter roared, sweeping the pots from the water barrel as he struggled drunkenly.

"She's your wife. She bore your four children." Papa said. "God will punish you!"

Fanya sobbed loudly, bent behind Mama's back.

"Yes? God will punish me?" Peter wobbled and dropped his fists. "Ptooey!" he spat over his shoulder, "Keep her then. I don't want her." He turned and staggered out.

Mama helped the crying woman onto the bench and urged her to drink some tea.

"I only wanted money for food," Fanya wept. "He took it all and then he hit me."

"Sha, sha." Mama smoothered her hair. "He'll get over it. He'll forget."

"Ah, Moshka," Fanya sobbed, "God bless you, you're a good man. No matter what they tell us about Jews, you're a good man."

"What do they tell you, Fanya?" Elli asked in surprise.

"Who tells you?" Rifka added a question.

"Ach, at the tavern, strangers come, they tell us bad things, but not about you, Moshka, you're a *good* Jew."

Mama and Papa exchanged uneasy glances.

"Eat your supper, children," Mama said sharply.

Summer was the time for picking strawberries and gooseberries with Raizelleh. Rifka's freckles grew darker and her dark hair turned a reddish blonde. One week, she would help Mama boil and preserve jugs of fruit jam; another week, they would cut chunks of red watermelon or small, tender cucumbers or the early tomatoes into wooden barrels filled with pickling spices and water. The best hours were spent with a book in the field or by the river.

One morning Elli and Zev got giddy on breaths of sunfilled air and turned down to the Savrankeh instead of up to Reb Mendl's for school. They waded and splashed in the river for a while, trying to catch fish in their skull caps. After eating lunch, they decided to be wild American Indians and went sneaking through the woods looking for people to capture. The murmur of voices coming from a clump of pine trees stirred their hunting instincts and they crept closer. Soon they could make out the words and clapped their hands to their mouths to keep from laughing out loud.

My beloved spoke and said to me,

Rise up my love, my fair one, and come away.

For lo, the winter is past,

The rain is over and gone,

The flowers appear on the earth.

They wiggled closer yet and discovered, to their great joy, that they had come upon Rifka and Leibel sprawled on the pine needles side by side, reading aloud to each other.

"Aiyeeee! Aiyeeeoh!" they jumped out, whooping ferociously, and fell on their startled quarry. There was a wild
melee of flying pine cones, thrashing feet, pebbles, and earth.
When the dust finally settled, Zev and Elli were being firmly
sat on by Leibel and Rifka.

"Get off!" screeched Elli, "or I'll tell Mama you were all
alone with a boy and you were reading about 'beloveds'!"

"That was the Bible, you dumbhead! And just for that I'll
tell Mama you played hookey from school," Rifka yelled.
"But first I'll pull your hair, you nosy little, pesky..."

"Rifka, stop — don't be mad. We found you by accident."

"Honest, Leibel," Zev chimed in, "We were just playing
Indian. Now, get off, you're squashing me!"

The older ones rolled off, Elli and Zev sat up, and they all looked at each other's scratched faces and hair prickly with pine needles, and began to laugh.

"All right, let's declare a truce," Leibel said. "Nobody tells anybody anything. Agreed?"

"Agreed."

"And anybody who breaks the truce..." he made a snarling face and shook his fist, "I'll grease him up and dust him with flour and bake him in my oven!"

The agreement was solemnly sealed by breaking Leibel's last roll into four pieces and sharing it.

Shayndel came home on a muggy day in the middle of August. Hirsh's horses trudged into town, dripping wet. Shayndel's uncle rushed up the steps from the drug store to help his niece down from the wagon.

The air was so thick that even the fat, black flies sat lazy and listless on the herring barrels, but somehow the news made its ways through the town. Soon the little store was crowded with customers who wanted two groschen worth of dried raspberries or four groschen of snuff, but most of all wanted to catch a glimpse of Shayndel.

"No, no." The druggist turned them away. "Shayndel has to rest. She's tired. She's sick. Haven't we had enough trouble already? Please, buy what you need and leave us alone."

Rifka had dropped her work and come running when she heard the news, but now she climbed up the steps from the store as disappointed as the rest. Suddenly she heard a "pssst" from the window above. A hand reached between the drawn curtains and motioned toward the side door. She ducked in quickly and found herself at the bottom of a flight of steps. Waiting at the top, with her arms spread wide, was Shayndel.

But what a different Shayndel! The dimples were gone, her cheeks were thin, there were dark hollows under her brown eyes — lifeless eyes, like burned-out candles.

They hugged and squeezed till they were both breathless, and when they moved apart, Rifka cried, "You got smaller! What did they do to you?"

"No," Shayndel smiled. "You got bigger — in just three months."

She paused for a minute and then went on, "As for what they did, I can't talk about it now. When I can, I will."

"Oh." Rifka suddenly didn't know what to say next, or what to do with her hands and feet. Those three months seemed to stand between them like a wall.

"I'm, I'm very happy you're home," Rifka finally said. "I've been waiting and missing you. And if you want, when you can, maybe you'll want to work with me and help me get ready for the test."

Shayndel shook her head. "No Rifka, I was afraid you'd ask me, but it's too late. It's hopeless. There are only three weeks before the high school examination in Belta, and that's not enough time to prepare."

"Try me," Rifka said boldly, her eyes bright with excitement. "I worked hard. It was the only way I could think of to help you — even though it was for me, not for you — still, it was like carrying on some of your work, wasn't it?"

"You mean you went ahead on your own?" Shayndel's face came alive. "Oh, Rifkalleh, then we may make it after all! We'll do it, we'll do it yet! What a victory that would be, to get you into high school in spite of them, in spite of my being in jail."

"As big a victory as getting a constitution?" Rifka asked, teasing.

"Bigger!" Shayndel laughed, and her eyes sparkled and her cheeks were pink again for a minute.

FIFTEEN

The Examination

Late summer became a frenzied study time. Rifka had to be not only good, but the absolute best. Because of the quota, only a small number of Jewish students would be allowed to pass the examination.

Everyone helped. Shayndel taught her, Leibel helped her drill the answers, Papa sewed writing books together and sharpened pen quills, Mama shortened and took in her own best black blouse for Rifka to wear to Belta, and Elli, Moozeleh, and the kids listened patiently to her memorizing.

When the great day finally came, the whole family — two-legged and four-legged — started for the marketplace together.

Berelleh came running after them, tripping on his night shirt, until Aunt Miriam snatched him back and gave Rifka a smoothering "good luck" kiss.

Raizelleh padded out barefoot and pushed some sugar candies into Rifka's pocket. "For the trip," she said. "If you're eating, you won't get nervous. Don't be scared, you're smart enough for the university already."

People in the marketplace called out to her.

"Good luck Rifkalleh."

"Show them we're not so dumb in Savran."

Even Hannah waved, while keeping one hand over her

vegetables and a wary eye on the goats. "A head like a prime minister — she'll make it."

Rifka blushed and nodded and felt like a puny David going into battle against Goliath for the honor of the town of Savran.

When they reached the wagon, Mama hugged her, retied her hair ribbons, and hugged again. Papa kissed her on the forehead and said, "Remember, Rifkalleh, passing or failing this examination will only matter for a little while. God is our only true judge and His standards are the ones we have to struggle to reach."

"Let's go already," Hirsh called. "What do you think, you're sending her to America? In two days, she'll be back. Stand back, everybody."

Rifka waved to her small family, but her eyes slid away, hunting, and just as the wheels began to turn, she saw Leibel running, his earlocks flying and his baker's apron flapping. "For you." He thrust a warm, yeasty-smelling bundle up at her and their hands met and squeezed and parted. "Be successful," he called as the wagon rattled out of the market-place and headed down the road to Belta.

Rifka spent a restless night at Fraydeh's house. Early next morning, a friend of Shayndel's in a short jacket, a shorter beard, and no earlocks banged the door knocker. Reb Sender glared at him over his glasses — this was clearly a godless young man — and reluctantly called Rifka. She was as white as her notebook paper and her stomach was flip-flopping like a freshly caught flounder.

"Now remember," the young man said as they walked, "don't mumble. Hold your head up — but not too high.

Don't talk about politics. If they ask you about socialism or democracy or about a constitution, say you don't know, you didn't study that."

Buildings swam by on both sides, people, wagons, even a put-putting automobile, but Rifka couldn't focus on anything but the churning mess of facts in her head.

Suddenly, too soon, she heard him say, "Here we are."

A massive stairway loomed before her, leading up to a gaping black entrance with grey stone columns at each side.

"Go on in, good luck." He shook her hand solemnly. "Go!" he shoved her and she started up.

The air in the long, dark hall was cold and damp. Rifka shivered even in the high, ruffled collar and long sleeves of her fine new blouse. She jumped when a small boy in a brass-buttoned, high-collared student's uniform popped out of a doorway.

"For the examination?" he asked.

She nodded.

"In here."

She entered a large, brightly-lit room, filled with rows of benches at which a few boys and girls sat. At the front, behind a large desk, stood a tall, broad-shouldered woman. A silver crucifix glittered on the pleated bosom of her dark dress. The thick braids of hair wrapped around her head were the same steel gray color as her eyes. A man in a high collar with a large blue nose sat directly behind her.

"Your papers?" the gray lady asked coldly.

Rifka handed her the letter Shayndel had written. She waited, feeling the eyes of the other students examining her curiously, feeling the clumsiness of her Savran-made shoes, wondering if her hair ribbons had come untied....

"Very well, Rifka Zelikovich of Savran, we'll begin with you," said the icy voice, and before Rifka could gulp a breath, her examiner began to snap rapid questions on Russian language, literature and history. Rifka found herself flinging the answers back — a little breathlessly, and not loud enough at first, but easily. As they continued, her voice became more sure. It's going all right, I really know all this, she thought with delighted surprise. But the teacher's lips drew tighter and tighter as the examination continued.

Finally, she paused to speak to the blue-nosed man, who clamped his spectacles on and stared at Rifka.

Maybe, Rifka wondered crazily, it's the pinching of the eye glasses that makes his nose blue.

The woman turned back and began to ask questions on geography. But her voice had changed. It had been cold and indifferent, but now it was like a hammer, slamming out question after question, almost without waiting for an answer. Rifka named rivers, cities, mountain ranges... but she had the puzzling feeling that her examiner wasn't really listening. Then the teacher asked, "Where is the United States?"

"The United States is in the Western hemisphere, in North America."

"And what kind of government does the United States have?"

"A democracy."

"What is a democracy?"

Alarm bells began to ring inside Rifka's head. "A, a democracy is a form of government where the people choose representatives to make laws."

"And what do you think of such a form of government?" The cold, gray eyes bored into the wide, blue ones. "You like it, don't you?"

"I, I d-don't know," Rifka said uneasily.

"You don't know? What kind of student are you? You've studied a form of government and you don't even have an opinion on it?"

"I don't know enough about it."

"I don't know enough about it," the teacher mimicked her.

"Well, you can't expect to pass an examination when you don't know enough about your subjects. You're dismissed. Wait outside. We'll let you know."

A soft mumur rose, as if all the waiting students had sighed at once, and their eyes followed her as she stumbled out the door.

"How did you do?" Shayndel's friend jumped up from the curb where he had been sitting and reading a newspaper.

"It was fine," she whispered through trembling lips. "I knew all the answers, every one, until the end. And then she asked me about democracy, and I didn't know what to say... and she..." her voice choked off and she squeezed her fists and eyes shut to keep from crying.

"Ptooey!" He spat fiercely and thrust the newspaper into his pocket. "They must have filled their quota of Jews and they needed an excuse to fail you. They should all grow like onions with their heads in the ground and their feet in the air! They don't want to give us a chance to breathe! Well, don't you worry," he patted her shoulder. "Just spit in their faces. Better times are coming." His voice dropped to a whisper. "Very soon, we'll have a constitution and a new government and they'll be begging for bright, eager students like you. Be patient."

"Come on now," he continued, taking her arm. "I'll take you home."

"No, she said to wait."

He shook his head pityingly and sat down again with his newspaper.

Rifka leaned against the railing. Her knees ached. So this was it. All the months of study, the goose money for books,

Papa's hard-earned groschen to pay for Shayndel's work-
— all wasted.

How could she go home? How could she face Shayndel?
How could she tell Papa and Mama she had failed? And
Raizelleh and Leibel? I'm nothing now, she thought.

The little student appeared in the doorway.

"Rifka Zelikovich?" he asked.

Rifka straightened up.

"Failed," he said.

SIXTEEN

No Answer from Above

It was almost the end of Yom Kippur, the day of reckoning of the Jewish year. The adult Jews of Savran had been fasting since sundown of the day before.

Blue twilight crept across the synagogue hall. Men swayed wearily to the chanting of the prayers. The great heavenly book with its verdicts of life and death for the year to come was closing with the sinking of the sun.

Elli clumped up the staircase to the women's balcony. "Rifka, I'm fainting from hunger," he whispered pitifully. "I think my stomach shrank into a raisin and I swallowed it. I can't wait another second."

"Nobody told you to fast," she snapped, annoyed at being interrupted in the middle of an important talk with God. "You're not old enough."

"I had to, I wanted to pray extra hard for Samson. He followed me to the synagogue today."

"Oh Elli, I'm sorry. I forgot. His time will be up soon."

"Don't say that," Elli wailed.

"The sun is almost gone. Go out and watch the sky. When you can see three stars, it'll be time to blow the shofar and then we'll all go home and eat."

"I'll never make it," he groaned. Clutching his stomach, he made his way through the swaying women to the staircase.

Rifka peeked down into the synagogue hall. The candles burned bright gold in the darkening room and the eternal flame above the Ark of Torah scrolls gleamed. But she wasn't ready for Yom Kippur to be over. She had come to have it out with God. Since her awful, tear-soaked trip home from Belta after the exam, she had been waiting to talk this out with God. And today, when the prayers of all the Jewish people from all over the world, even from Velvl in America, were flying up to heaven together, today He would have to listen.

So Rifka had fasted and prayed. She didn't leave her seat all day, not even in the middle of the afternoon when most people went out for a nap or a breath of fresh autumn air. In between the formal prayers, she told Him about the test and the terrible gray lady, about Shayndel, about her hopes to go to school, to do important work, to help people — and how none of that would happen now.

Why should that be, she asked. Was it â bad thing to want? Hadn't she worked hard? Was it fair that she should fail the examination? What reason could He possibly have?

The light at the synagogue windows was darkening from deep blue to blue-black. The quiet drone of prayer came alive. The congregation was standing, alert and straining. In one voice, they called, "Hear, oh, Israel, the Lord our God, the Lord is One!"

"Oh no," Rifka cried silently, "Not yet. I'm not ready. He didn't answer me yet!"

The voices grew stronger and happier as they recited the Kaddish prayer in praise of God, and then hushed as the sexton cried out thinly, "Tekeeya!"

The blower's cheeks bulged and his face turned red, as he sounded the notes of the ram's horn over the heads of the congregation.

For better or for worse, the five thousand, six hundred and sixty-sixth year of the Jewish calendar had begun.

Elli was the last one left at the table.

He thought he would never fill the hole left by the Yom Kippur fast. After the stuffed fish and the noodles with cheese, he began on the beet soup and potatoes. When he finished all the potatoes, he asked for a little more potato to finish the borsht, and then just a little more borsht to finish the potato, and then a little more potato..... This could have gone on until Hanukkah, but he was interrupted in the middle of a spoonful by the noise of loud hammering right outside the kitchen door.

In the yard, he saw the shadowy figures of Papa and Rifka, measuring and lifting boards. As he watched, Rifka held a board up between the fence post and the kitchen door frame. Papa hammered it into place.

"The Sukkah!" Elli cried, gulping down his potato. "You're starting to build the Sukkah. I want to help!"

Immediately after Yom Kippur, each Jewish family in Savran began to build its Sukkah — a small open-roofed hut in which they would celebrate the Sukkos holiday. Papa and Rifka had started work earlier than any of their neighbors.

Elli ran out eagerly, but they barely noticed him. They were deep in talk.

"No, God does not have to answer to us for everything that happens," Papa was saying. "We have to trust in His wisdom and justice, even when we can't understand it."

"But it's not right. Why should He let bad things happen if He's so good and so strong? What good is all our praying to Him if bad things keep happening?"

"We don't pray to ask favors of God. We pray for our own sake. Prayer draws the uncleanness out of us the same way as salt draws uncleanness out of Kosher meat. If the world is bad, it's because people themselves are at fault."

Rifka was shaking her head, but Papa continued steadily.

"We have to work to make ourselves better people. Geography, grammar, constitutions, money — none of these can bring a better world..."

"No, no, no!" Rifka broke in, "I'm as good as I know how to be, and I tried so hard. He should've helped me. He's not fair! He's wrong!"

"Rifkalleh, sha! You don't know what you're saying." Her father's brows pulled together angrily, but his eyes were sad.

She threw down her board and ran into the house.

For another hour, Elli and a silent, troubled Papa worked together and finished building the framework of the small room leaning against the outside wall of the kitchen. Its walls were a strange patchwork of Mama's long noodle cutting board, the shed ladder, and parts of an old fence, with two barrels wedged into the gaps. Its roof was only a crisscross of branches open to the sun, moon, stars, and rain. Later in the week, they would add reeds from the riverbank and hang fruits, vegetables, and flowers for decoration.

Fanya came by the next afternoon on her way to the well. Elli was wobbling on a bench, tying radishes and onions to the roof branches, and kicking Samson away so the goat wouldn't gobble up the vegetable decorations.

"Hey, Fanya," he called, "Do you know anybody who needs a strong, nice, handsome billy goat? But he has to be a good person."

"Tch, tch. There are too many billy goats in this world already," she said, "but I'll ask around."

She watched him for a minute and then shrugged. "Who understands you people... building a room with a worthless roof."

"That's how we want it," Elli hurried to explain. "So we should feel like we're living out in the field in the middle of the harvest season in the Land of Israel. It's for the Sukkos holiday next week."

"Why do you play at it? If you want to be farmers, come and work in the field like my family does."

"Papa says they won't let us. The Czar made a law that Jews aren't allowed to be farmers."

She slapped her side and laughed. "For us peasants, he made a law that we *must* be farmers and must work on the same land that our fathers worked. Well, I suppose the Little Father knows what's best." She started off again, laughing to herself, and then called back, "I'll bring you some old carrots tomorrow to decorate your holy roof."

"Rifka!" Elli jumped down and ran into the kitchen. "Fanya is going to find a peasant who wants Samson, and she's going to bring us carrots for the Sukkah, too, and it looks beautiful already. Come help me finish."

Rifka had tucked herself into the corner between the table and the heating wall, intent on her embroidery. "No," she said without looking up.

"What's the matter? Are you mad at me?"

"No. You're all right."

"Who then?"

"I can't say. Go away."

"Mama?"

"No. Someone more important."

"Who could be more important?"

"Leave me alone. Can't you see I'm busy?" she yelled.

"Well, why should *I* do all the work."

"Then don't, just leave me alone!" she slammed her embroidery down and stormed into the bedroom.

Rifka stormed and stamped and glowered like a thundercloud during the next few days. She collected eggs, milked, pitted plums for pickling, and helped take care of Berelleh and Meyer—all in a blur of hot, angry, unshed tears.

Mama watched and worried.

"Give her a few good slaps," Aunt Miriam advised. "Then she'll have a good cry and get it out of her system."

"No, she needs time. It's like, heaven forbid, she's sitting *shivah*, the seven days of mourning."

"What? Mourning for high school?"

"Mourning for her dreams."

Shayndel came one afternoon. "It wasn't your fault that you failed. It was the quota. Better times are coming very soon. Leibel's brother is out of jail, our work is succeeding. You'll take the examination again and you'll pass."

But Rifka bit her lip and turned away.

Leibel whistled outside the window in the evening. Rifka recognized his tall, gawky shadow and ducked down over her sewing, pretending not to hear.

She didn't want anybody. She didn't know what she *did* want right then except maybe to throw rocks at the grey lady, or the Czar, or...she didn't dare think further.

And the storm inside Rifka had a gigantic, terrifying echo in the cities and over the huge countryside of Russia that autumn. Shayndel and Sasha and their many comrades had called up the storm clouds and now lightening and thunder was shaking the land.

In faraway Moscow, a strike of printers and bakers began. The next day, factory workers joined the strike. They surged through the streets of Moscow, shouting for shorter workdays and free elections. Strikes broke out like smallpox in other cities all across the country. Thousands of people were arrested and beaten. Cossacks on horseback charged into crowds, trampling and whipping, but still the epidemic spread. Even the peasants began to revolt, setting their dogs on the tax collectors. "The land is ours now," they said simply. "We won't pay."

Anxious people waited at the Savran post office, until the newspapers were opened and read. Hirsh the wagon driver was surrounded as soon as he clattered into town, even before he could climb down from the wagon.

"In Odessa, there is a blonde young man," he told his listeners one day. "Skinny, long-legged like a spider, appears from nowhere, makes fiery speeches about strikes, constitutions, gets the crowds gabbling like a flock of geese, and then scurries away one step ahead of the police. A spider!"

Sasha! Rifka thought, hurrying past.

Despite the rumbling of revolution, the tomatoes and watermelons ripened in the fields, leaves of willows and birches yellowed, and the oaks showed a hint of red. The marketplace was heaped with cabbages, melons, carrots, and pumpkins, ready to be pickled or stored for the coming winter. And the long-legged storks fished busily near the washerwomen, filling up for their yearly trip south.

The harvest holiday of Sukkos was ending. All week, the

family had eaten in the small Sukkah under the hanging vegetable decorations with sunlight filtering through the open
roof. This was the last day. This morning, the final chapter
of the Torah would be read in the synagogue and then the
Bible scroll would be rerolled to its beginning and the reading would begin all over again with chapter one, the story of
Genesis.

Papa and Elli left early. After Mama and Rifka had fed
the goats and chickens, Mama put on her silk holiday kerchief and came out to the steps where Rifka sat gloomily,
scratching Moozeleh's shaggy neck.

"You like Moozeleh a whole lot, don't you?" she asked,
sitting down close beside her.

Rifka nodded.

"Can you imagine ever doing anything to hurt her — for no
good reason?"

"Oh no." Rifka ran her hand fondly along the goat's velvet
ear and Moozeleh nuzzled her neck.

"Papa and I love you too, Rifkalleh. And you know we
would never do anything to harm you."

"I know."

"And God is the parent of us all. Can you believe He would
do anything to hurt any of us unless there was good reason?"

"Oh, Mama, I just don't know. I don't know anything anymore." The stored up tears spilled over and ran down her
cheeks.

Mama waited.

Finally, Rifka blew her nose and sighed. "I, I don't think
He would," she said. "I don't want to think so!"

"I'm glad."

They watched the chickens scratching for worms in the

holiday-quiet road. Moozeleh flopped on her side and dozed off beside them. The door across the street banged open and Uncle Ephraim ran down the steps, carrying his Prayer Book and shawl.

"Good holiday, I'm late," he gasped, and ran on.

"It's time for me to go, too." Mama got up and brushed off her skirt.

"Me, too," Rifka said, feeling relieved and happy. She took a flying leap over Moozeleh and seized her mother's hand.

Clapping and singing people spilled out on the street in front of the synagogue. On this joyous holiday, even the women and girls came down from the balcony and joined the men so they could kiss the Torah scrolls that the men carried, circling around and around the synagogue seven times. Each man and older boy had a turn at carrying a scroll in the procession. The younger ones, like Elli and Berelleh, skipped beside their fathers.

"Rifkalleh, Rifkalleh!" Raizelleh ran toward her, squealing with excitement. They threw their arms around each other.

"I thought you'd never come out again, I'm so happy. I have so much to tell you."

"Oh, Raizelleh, I missed you, too."

Squeezing hands, they pressed into the synagogue and moved forward to reach the procession of Torah scrolls.

Reb Lazer the water carrier was just dancing past with a little skip like Samson the kid's, his grizzled beard pressed against the gold embroidered cover and his eyes half closed with joy. After him, came Reb Nissen the butcher, strutting like a rooster, hugging the scrolls to his chest and happily bellowing the prayer, "Oh Lord, answer us when we call to

you...." Then Reb Chayim the cloth merchant passed with a mincing dance step that made the fringes of his prayer shawl shimmy, bellowing even louder to a completely different tune. One after another, the men went by, dreaming, lost in their joy and love for the holy Scrolls.

Rifka kept stretching on her tiptoes and searching. Finally, on the fifth round of the procession, Leibel's fiery head appeared above the crowd. She leaned forward happily, wanting to touch him but only daring to kiss the Bible he carried. His eyes popped, his mouth dropped open, and he stopped short. Shloimeh the carpenter, stepping gaily along behind, ploughed right into him. Reb Fishkeh, who came next, almost climbed up on top of both of them in a bumping mix-up of bruised noses and shins. Fortunately, in such a crowd there was no room for anybody to fall down, but it took several verses of singing before all the bells and tassles and prayer shawls were untangled.

"This is why women belong in the balcony!" Shloimeh blustered and glared at Rifka and Raizelleh before he continued around the synagogue.

"Wait for me later," Leibel said and hurried on.

At last, the circling was done. One by one, all the scrolls except two were put back into the Holy Ark. The singing and stamping quieted, as the men settled into their places and the women and girls climbed up the steps to the balcony.

One scroll was unrolled to the final chapter of Deuteronomy, the last book of the Torah.

Rifka settled down to listen. This was a sad one, she remembered — Moses climbing up the mountain to die by himself, not being allowed to cross into the Promised Land. Was that fair? After forty years in the desert? Did Moses stamp around on the mountain top and argue about fairness the way she would? She had to giggle at the thought.

You shall see the land from far away,
but you shall not go to the land
which I give to the children of Israel...

Loud cries from the doorway broke into the sing-song reading.

"Stop!"

"Listen to us!"

The women flattened their noses against the lattice to see better.

"It's not a time for prayer. It's a time for action!" the voices below shouted.

"Shame! Out — get out!" other voices sounded.

"Come on! Let's see what's happening." Raizelleh yanked Rifka to the stairs.

"We have a right to speak in the synagogue, just as you do!" A strong voice blasted up the stairwell.

Four young men and tight lipped, white-faced Shayndel with them stood in the entrance surrounded by an indignant circle of worshippers who were trying to push them out the door.

"That's Dov!" Rifka cried. "Leibel's brother Dov."

The pushers fell back as the white-bearded Rabbi came to face the group of young people. He was a small man, his head reached only as high as Dov's shoulder, but with his shaggy eyebrows drawn and his silver beard jutting forward commandingly he forced everybody to step back.

"What can be important enough to interrupt the Torah reading?" the Rabbi demanded sternly.

"This is a matter of life and death," Dov answered, "We have a right to speak."

"No! They'll bring the police down on us," others shouted and began to push again.

"Any Jew has a right to be heard in the synagogue," the Rabbi quieted the crowd. "Speak quickly so that we can finish the Bible reading."

Dov walked through the congregation and climbed the steps to the reading desk. He looked strangely out of place wearing a cap and ragged sweater instead of a prayer shawl.

"People of Savran," he began, "Russia is rising in a revolution. Workers and peasants, teachers and students, Jews and Christians are raising the red flag. We're demanding freedom, a constitution, justice.

"This is no time to hide behind prayers and holidays. We have to join the people's struggle. If the Hebrew prophets were alive today, they would be standing here with me. Put down your prayer books, join the..."

"Blasphemer, liar, atheist!" A burly man cried out hoarsely. He jumped up with tears running down his cheeks and rushed toward the reading platform. "My own son, oh, my own son!"

The Rabbi blocked the steps and others hurried to hold the baker back.

Dov stopped speaking and his face twisted as though he would cry, but then he slammed his fist on the desk instead, so hard that the lamp above quivered. "Listen to me!" he cried. "The revolution is here. You must join it or be destroyed by it." He rushed past his struggling father and out into the bright autumn sunshine.

The reader's voice chanting the Bible reading sounded

above the hubbub. Slowly, the congregation quieted down, except for the baker's muffled sobs, as the scroll was read to the end. Then the reader began again in the yearly cycle from the first verse of Genesis, that would continue as long as the Jewish people would live.

In the beginning, God created the heaven and the
   earth.
And the earth was confusion
And darkness was upon the face of the deep....

SEVENTEEN

Elli's Rescue

Elli had seen the quick look that passed between his mother and his father when he filled the pail for Samson's supper last night. He had been waiting for it. A useless eater, the look said. He'll never give milk, he'll just eat and eat right through the winter when there is barely enough food for the family. The holidays are over. It's time.

The little boy woke in a panic remembering the look. It was nearly morning. He could hear the sleepy waking up calls of the birds through the window. Elli inched himself off the bed, pulled on his pants and warm shirt, and tiptoed out. Papa's heavy breathing was the only sound in the quiet, pre-dawn house. Inch by inch, the boy pushed the door open. Good — he was out. Suddenly, from the shed, Kvetcher crowed a triumphant "good morning." Nobody heard but Elli and a few chickens.

The goats were asleep in a warm, furry heap. Their sides rose and fell, breaths sweet with fresh clover and carrot greens. Gently, Elli slipped a rope around the black-and-white goat's neck and then poked him with his toe. Samson opened an eye, stretched his hind legs, and curled up again.

Elli was ready. He had saved a chunk of fresh pumpkin, Samson's favorite food. He held it under the goat's nose and poked again. This time, Samson opened both yellow eyes

152

wide and then scrambled up to follow the food out through the shed door. Elli drew him through the gate, shut it quietly, and let him nibble the pumpkin as they started down the dark street. Blank windows stared at them. Heavy silence hung over the straw roofs and cold chimneys.

"Ssssh," he hissed at clattering Samson and shivered fearfully. Suddenly, there was a yowling shriek from an alley and a gray shadow hurtled by.

Just a cat. Elli's teeth were chattering. Maybe I'll go home now, and later I'll ask Zev to come with me, he thought.

A light flickered yellow in the window beside him and another rooster crowed. Too late. Papa will be getting up already.

He grabbed Samson's rope more tightly and began to run. They raced through the sleeping marketplace, down the road leading to the Savrankeh River, and out across the small bridge.

"I know you don't understand where we're going, Samson," Elli told the goat as their feet clumped on the wooden boards, "But you're my friend. I'm practically your godfather because I even saw you getting born, and I can't let Reb Nissen butcher you. Even though I agreed at the Passover Seder, and

Papa is going to be mad at me, it would be like, like sending my brother to the butcher." He hunched up his shoulders and buttoned his shirt up to his chin. It was cold.

Dawn was breaking through the gray sky ahead. Mist rising from the fields glowed pink with the first rays of the sun. Elli began to feel braver.

"We're going to walk and walk," he said loudly, "and we'll stop at each peasant's house and ask if they want a boy goat. You're so strong and handsome, somebody is going to want you. Someplace somebody's billy goat must've just died."

"Mm-eh, eh, eh," said Samson, tugging his head aside for a quick bite of grass.

A patch of woods lay ahead. As they entered, the glimmer of dawn disappeared and they were in darkness again. Elli's steps were muffled by the fallen leaves but Samson clip-clopped loudly enough to bring out the whole czarist army, or at least all the bears, wolves, lions, and other wild animals that might live in the woods. Elli was not clear about what lived in the forest — he had spent most of his childhood in Reb Mendl's schoolroom — but he knew it was a dangerous place.

He began to run again. Samson galloped beside him, pleased with this new game, and soon pink daylight showed ahead and the road appeared between the fields again.

"There's a house, Samson," Elli cried.

The house huddled low and dark against the gold sky and its thatched roof almost blended with the tall stalks of corn around it. As the boy and the goat came closer, they heard the barking of a dog from inside. Elli hesitated. That sounded like a big dog, and he didn't know about dogs. Only peasants had dogs. But what could he do? He was more afraid of going back into the woods than of going forward.

"C-come on Samson." He walked shakily up to the low wooden door. Before he could knock, there was a scuffle from within and then a powerful thump that almost knocked the door from its hinges, and then more barking.

Elli and Samson sprang back and took off down the road. They ran and ran until the sound of the barking was left behind.

Elli slowed to a stumble. His stomach was hurting. He was sure they'd been walking for hours and he hadn't asked even one person if he needed a billy goat. He sat down and let Samson hunt for breakfast in the field. Well, he thought, at least I don't have to milk him. Idiot—he answered himself—if you had to milk Samson, you wouldn't have a problem.

A man and a boy, both barefoot and carrying baskets, came down the road toward him.

"Good morning, God be with you," they greeted him politely, but with puzzled glances. "Are you lost?"

He jumped up eagerly. "Do you need a male goat? Just to be a father. I mean not for meat."

The man smiled. "We have pigs, no goats. Petya has goats." He pointed ahead.

Petya's house had a muddy yard where a dozen chickens and four goats rummaged. Two little blonde children stood in the doorway, sucking their fingers. Elli looked over them into a small, dark room where straw mattresses lay piled against the walls and a woman worked by the cooking fire in the corner.

"Good morning," he said timidly, "would you want a male goat? Not to eat, just to have. See, he's really beautiful."

She came to the door shaking her head. "We have a male. Are you lost, little boy?" She looked at him curiously. "Are you hungry?"

"No." Elli gulped and turned away.

By now, Mama would have cooked chicory with milk and boiled potatoes for breakfast, and his school lunch would be ready, a chunk of cheese, a pickle, white bread left from the holiday...he sighed. Samson, behind him, was ripping up grass enthusiastically.

"Do you have to make so much noise?" Elli grumbled, and then tried a mouthful of grass himself.

"Ssspltch!" He spat it out.

The next small whitewashed house was surrounded by bushy tomato plants still carrying a few late fall fruits. Elli's stomach jiggled with interest. He looked around carefully, then bent and picked a big, ripe tomato.

Suddenly, a cloud of dust appeared ahead on the road. A horse and wagon rumbled out of the cloud toward them. Elli spluttered and choked on his stolen tomato. He spun around and dragged Samson back, leaping over the plants in a wild panic, stumbling and tripping until he fell into a hedgerow separating two fields. The wagon screeched and rattled to a stop at the path leading up to the house.

"Come out Ivan...Katya!" Elli heard the driver shout. He peered through the bush. The driver was standing up in his seat, waving his cap, and shouting again, "Come out, there's news!"

Two children raced around from the back of the house. A man carrying a hoe followed them.

"Drop your tools! It's a holiday today. No work. We have a constitution! The little Father gave us a constitution!"

"Aaaiy Katya," Ivan roared and pounded on the door. "Did you hear? We have a constitution. That means the land is ours."

Happy shrieks came from inside. A big black dog bounded out the door, followed by his excited mistress.

"Bless the Little Father!"

"Come have a drink, we'll celebrate." Ivan waved to the wagon driver.

"No, come to town; we'll all celebrate. I have to let the others know."

The black dog charged down the path. He darted around the wagon and the children, sharing the excitement. Then he caught a strange new smell. The ruff of hair around his neck rose and a deep growl rumbled up from his belly. Nose to the ground, he padded along Elli and Samson's trail to the far edge of the field and squeezed through the hedge. To his surprise he found himself facing Samson's dangerously lowered head and dagger-sharp horns.

"What's he after? A rabbit?" The voices beyond the hedge came faintly.

The dog barked, backed away, and circled slowly, just out of reach of the stabbing horns.

"A rabbit! Get him!" the children shrilled.

Elli huddled back under the bush behind the goat, frozen with fear, unable to open his mouth.

Constitution! Constitution!

Papa heard the cry when he ran down the road to the river, but he was too busy searching the shore, to pay attention. He could think only of Elli. He had to find Elli.

The family had not missed him until breakfast time. Rifka ran to Zev's house looking for him. She ran to the school and out to the meadow by the clay pit where Elli loved to play. Mama pulled on her shawl and ran across the road to ask Uncle Ephraim to help in the search, and then hurried to the marketplace to ask each of the peddlers and shopkeepers if they had seen Elli pass. Ephraim hurried in the opposite direction. He gritted his teeth, climbed the steps and peeked timidly into the dark, incense-smelling hall of the church, and nearly tumbled down backwards when a black-robed priest appeared to ask what he wanted.

Rifka got home first and found Moozeleh bawling with hunger and discomfort, waiting to be milked. It was only then, when the two females rushed to her, that she noticed Samson was gone. Immediately she realized what must have happened. Elli had run away with Samson. She herself had done the same thing once when she was afraid that Moozeleh was to be butchered.

Think, think, where could Samson and Elli have gone?

She filled the food pails and set out the milk pail. Skwitch, skwitch, skwitch...her hands squeezed the goat's warm teats as the milk foamed into the pail.

What was it he had said about Fanya? Fanya would find a home for Samson...Skwitch, skwitch...with a peasant!

That's it! Elli had gone into the countryside to the peasants.

She must find Papa. She finished milking quickly and ran out through the streets to the marketplace.

But what was happening?

Even as she ran, she noticed strange things. Reb Leib's wife and maid were standing on the balcony tying a great, rippling red sheet to the railing.

"Rifka!" they called out, "Constitution!"

Little boys darted in a pack up and down the porches, waving bits of red cloth and yelling.

Why weren't they at school? Where were all the carts and wagons on the street? She saw only people — looking out of windows, calling, hurrying into the street, running beside her. The marketplace was humming with people. She turned down another street to get to the river. Papa had said he would hunt for Elli there. To her great relief, she soon saw her father making his way toward her.

"Papa!" she cried, "I know where to look!"

At that moment, Elli would have given up a whole pocketfull of buttons to be safely back in Savran. The black dog was circling, his eyes flicking from Samson to Elli and back to Samson, making a strange, eager, whining sound. He backed away; his muscles tightened. He plunged forward in a lightning rush to pass Samson's horns and reach the boy behind him. The goat flipped his head and caught the dog in the ribs with one horn, flinging him to the side. The dog whined shrilly for a moment as he backed away and began to trot back and forth again, looking for an opening.

Elli forced his frozen jaws apart. "Help," he cried weakly.

Feet thudded across the field, and through the bushes. Elli heard voices yelling to drive off the dog, then the clatter of Samson's hooves as he was pulled away. A circle of surprised faces looked down at him.

Elli blinked in the sunlight. "W-w-would you like a f-fine, s-s-strong b-billy goat?" he stuttered feebly.

"That goat is a Cossack! He's better than a Cossack. He's a constitution goat! He saved your life, boy! My dog could've torn you to pieces," the driver roared. "I would be proud to own such a goat! But who are you? Where do you come from?"

"From Savran."

"You're a Jew?"

Elli nodded.

"Brother!" Ivan plucked him up and gave him a bone-crunching hug. "Today we're all brothers. Jews, Christians, peasants, storekeepers. We have a constitution today!"

The wagon driver swept Elli up and planted him on his shoulders. "I'll take you home to Savran," he laughed, "but first we'll spread the news."

Papa and Rifka had crossed the bridge, passed the first cleared field and now were crunching over the carpet of brown, red, and gold leaves leading through the patch of woods. The sun blazed though the autumn foliage; they were in a gold-lit tunnel of leaves.

Just ahead, they saw the low, thatched roof of the peasant hut poking above the corn stalks.

"Elli may have stopped here," Papa said. "If not, we'll have to go back and try and another direction." He sighed and his lips began to move in silent prayer.

Rifka shaded her eyes against the sun, looking for Samson's black-and-white coat, but seeing only a few moving dots — chickens.

Wagon wheels grated on the road beyond the turn. Soon the wagon itself came around and pulled to a stop. The driver stood up, and his voice stabbed through the still, clear air over the harvested fields.

"Stepan! Stepan! Come out, hear the news. Constitu-toooooootion!"

A small figure on the seat beside him stood up, too, and a little boy's voice rang out shrilly, "Constitoootion! Constitoootion!"

"Elli, Elli, Elli!" Rifka shrieked and ran toward the wagon.

"I thank you, God, oh, I thank You," Papa cried hoarsely and ran after her.

EIGHTEEN

"Constitoootion!"

"Jump on the wagon, friends!" the driver cried. "We're going to Savran to hear the Czar's proclamation and then we'll all celebrate."

Papa helped Stepan onto the seat, then he and Rifka scrambled over the side to join Elli and two others, as the wagon lurched off to Savran.

"A song in honor of the Little Father who is giving us freedom," the driver shouted and began to bawl a Russian army song.

The others joined in, shouting and clapping. Even Papa sang at the top of his lungs. Rifka hugged Elli and hugged Papa and felt as if she would burst for joy. Everything was working out, everybody was together — peasants, Jews, the Czar. Elli was found. Shayndel and Sasha had won their fight for a constitution. Everything was good, good, good!

"Hurray!" she shouted, punctuating the chorus of the song.

The driver tied up his horse before the crowded marketplace. Papa hurried off to find Mama and Ephraim to tell them Elli was found. He ordered Rifka not to let go of her wandering brother for one second and to budge no further than Chayim's cloth stand.

Rifka and Elli searched, but where was Chayim's stand? It must have been swept away by the shouting, laughing,

162

dancing people who flooded the marketplace. Red ribbons
sparkled on blouses and jackets—red, the color of the revolution. Young people rushed around handing out papers.

Shayndel pounced on Rifka and Elli. "We won, we won!"
she laughed, hugging them. "The future is open, we can do
anything now!"

Chayim, arm in arm with the druggist, stopped and
exuberantly pumped Shayndel's hand. "All you crazy young
people, nothings, no money, no influence, but you did it! I'm
proud of you."

Somehow Leibel found them in the great shoving crowd. Rifka hugged him, too, and he blushed.

"Everything is all right now, you see," Rifka bubbled. "Shayndel and Dov were right. I'm so glad."

But he shook his head. "We can't depend on others..." he began.

"Ssssh, quiet," people called. "The proclamation. The constitution proclamation."

Stumpy, broad-shouldered Fedka with the large, drooping mustache rose about the crowd, standing on a wagon and holding up a long sheet of paper.

"Hurray for the police! Hurray for Fedka! Hurray for the Czar!" cries arose.

Fedka smiled and smoothed his mustache, motioning for silence. He looked at his paper for a minute, until he remembered that he didn't know how to read. He pulled up beside him a tall, lean, young man wearing a worker's cap, with a shock of blond hair shadowing his deep-set eyes. "You read it," he growled and handed him the proclamation.

Sasha, Rifka thought uneasily. At critical times, Sasha always seemed to turn up.

Sasha began to read:

We, Nicholas the Second, by the grace of God, Emperor and Autocrat of all the Russias, declare that the agitation and troubles in our land fill our heart with pain. We seek only the well-being of our people. We direct our government to carry out our will in the following way:

First, to allow all the people freedom of speech, of thought, and of assembly.

Second, to allow all the people the right to vote.
Third, to give the legislature, elected by the people, the
   right to supervise the acts of our own ministers.
We appeal to all faithful sons of Russia to cooperate with
us in restoring calm and peace to our homeland.

The marketplace vibrated with a roar of approval: "Long
live the Czar!" "Long live the Little Father!" "Hurrah for the
constitution!"

Shayndel took Rifka's hand and spun her into a circle of
dancing people. Old and young—everyone joined in. Sasha
and Ivan skipped into the center, dropped to their haunches,
and danced the wild, kicking *kozatzkeh*, pulling against each
other for balance. People gathered, clapping, singing,
shouting—"hey, hey, hey!"—to the rhythm of the stamping
dance.

Up above, the October sun shone on the singing crowds,
the red ribbons, and the explosion of happiness and brother-
hood that had shaken Savran and all of Russia.

Rifka felt herself pulled from the circle. It was Papa. "Why
did you..." she began, but stopped at the sight of his pale,
strained face. Elli danced past and Papa seized him. He
pulled them both through the crowd. Here and there, he
stopped to say a quick word—to Chayim, to Hannah, to
Mendl — and went on, with his baffled children in tow.

"Now get home," he ordered them at the edge of the
marketplace. "Tell Mama I'll be back soon. I have to spread
the word."

"What word?"

"They're gathering the peasants to attack us. Fanya came
to warn us."

"They can't," Rifka cried, "there's a constitution now!"

"You're a child, you don't understand. Take Elli home right now." He left them and hurried away.

"Elli, I need your help." She turned to him desperately.

"Please go home by yourself. I have to speak to Shayndel and Sasha. I know they can stop this."

He nodded, his eyes large and frightened, and ran toward home.

Rifka plunged back into the holiday crowd. Faces were laughing and shouting on all sides, but she didn't see the one she was looking for. She made her way around to the druggist's shop. It was dark and locked. A flutter of color caught her eye, a red scarf hung from the window above the store. She ran to the side door and pounded on it, then pushed it open, and hurried up the stairs. Shayndel met her at the top.

"Rifka, you shouldn't burst in..." she began crossly.

But Rifka gave her no chance to go on. "Shayndel, Fanya told Papa that the peasants are going to start a pogrom! You and Sasha are heroes now—you have to stop them!"

"Fanya is wrong. They would never do that," Shayndel said hotly. "We're all together now, we're brothers. They know how we all fought together for this constitution. Just look," She pulled Rifka into the room and across to the window.

Rifka caught a quick glimpse of a long-legged young man sprawled on a bench in the corner. From the window, she could see the marketplace was still alive with circles of dancers, splashes of red ribbon, and flying pieces of white proclamation pamphlets. Snatches of songs floated up.

"You see, it's beautiful. How could you spread such an awful rumor, Rifkalleh?" Shayndel scolded her. "Now go home, please. Sasha is leaving for Odessa soon and we still have a lot of planning to do."

"I'm sorry. I didn't want to disturb—interfere—and I'm so happy about the constitution, and the Czar, and everything," Rifka babbled, feeling foolish and hurrying to get away from Sasha's deep, appraising eyes.

Halfway to the steps, she stopped. New cries sounded from the outside—fierce, electric cries.

Kill the Jews!
God bless the Little Father!
Down with the Jews!

Rifka whirled and ran back to the window. A group of men was moving along the street that led to the Belta road. The late afternoon sun gleamed on banners with the design of a two-headed eagle—the Czar's banner. Some were carrying pictures of the Czar.

The Jews steal from the people!
The Jews take our land!

Men were waving clubs, scythes, and pitchforks as they advanced into the marketplace. The crowds turned to face them in shocked silence. They shrank back. Shouts arose: "no, no...brotherhood...constitution...democracy." Someone threw a stone at the advancing group. They surged forward at a run, like a dark wave rolling over the colorful debris of the celebration, and piercing, wailing screams arose as mothers snatched up children, fathers herded their families, and old people stumbled and fell in their rush to get out of the marketplace.

"Sasha!" Shayndel choked out a cry and turned from the window. "We have to stop them. You can't go now!"

"I have to go. We have to work to get our people onto the election slate right now. The revolution depends on this."

"But they're going to kill our people out there. What good is the revolution?"

He put his hands on her shoulders and looked down into her eyes. "Shayndel, we have to make personal sacrifices to bring a better world. The peasants may kill a few Jews in a pogrom, but that's only a first step in their political education. After that, they'll realize that the landlords and the aristocrats are their true enemies, and after that, they'll be ready to turn on the Czar himself. And then, they'll be ripe and ready for socialism."

"No, that's not right!" she cried and twisted away from him. "You're ready to let innocent people be killed, my own people. And you call yourself my comrade, my good friend..." She stopped, remembering Rifka who stood silently, by the window.

"You don't understand. You're getting too emotional." Sasha's voice was soft, even sad, but it vibrated in the small bedroom. "If we work to cut down a forest, we must expect chips to fall."

"Am I a chip, too?" she whispered.

"Don't be silly," Sasha bristled.

"Come on, Rifka!" Shayndel grabbed Rifka's hand and pulled her to the steps. "I'll get you home and then I'll get people together and we'll stop this!"

NINETEEN

"Fire!"

Glass shattered shrilly when they were halfway down the steps. Two men were breaking through the window of the drug store.

"Stop! What are you doing?" Shocked, Shayndel recognized one of the thieves. "Aftod! We're friends. Why are you breaking in? If you need something and you can't pay, I'll give it to you."

"Oh, Shayndel, better go and hide." He pushed her back. "We have to do this. The man said, 'Beat the Jews, rob the Jews, it's for the Czar's sake.' I wouldn't touch a hair on your head, you're my friend, but the others don't know you. Hurry and hide."

"What man?" she demanded, pulling at his arm.

"A man at the tavern, a government man." He pulled away and climbed through the window after his friend.

"I'll call Fedka," Shayndel cried. "Police!"

Aftod's kindly, concerned face appeared at the window again. "Fedka went away. Better hide."

Shayndel and Rifka stared at each other helplessly.

"Hurry, we'll go to the bakery first. This way — through the side streets," Shayndel urged.

The street was empty and still. There were no children, no goats or chickens, even the cats seemed to be hiding. Here and there, people were working grimly, closing shutters and putting up door and window bars. From the marketplace, they heard unfamiliar sounds of banging, thumping, more shattering glass, and faint cries.

"When they finish with the marketplace, they'll start coming here, to people's houses," Shayndel panted. "I have to get Dov and Fyodr and the others, we'll stop the peasants before this spreads through the town."

At the bakery, young men were rolling barrels of flour against the doors as a barricade. Sticks, hammers, and shovels were piled in a corner. Leibel and his father were nailing the shutters closed. Dov was digging in the yard.

"We have three guns buried here," Dov said.

"Dov, no!" Shayndel was horrified. "The guns were only to be used against the soldiers or the Cossacks—not against the people. We have to talk to them...to explain...educate."

"Shayndel, we'll try to talk to them," Dov answered, "but if that doesn't work, we'll fight."

Shayndel's face was chalky but she took a stick and stood with him. Fyodr, the son of a peasant, clutched his gun and stood with his comrades, too. For him, this might be a harder day than for any of the others.

Leibel took the only remaining weapon—a rolling pin. "I'm coming, too." He ran to join them.

"No, no more, Dov is enough!" his mother cried.

"Stay out of this," Dov ordered him. "You're just a kid. Take Rifka home through the back streets and then hide and stay out of trouble."

"All right. Let's go."

The baker gripped Dov's arm as he passed, pulled him close and said gruffly, "God be with you—even though you're a revolutionary."

Rifka and Leibel went out the back door, dodged under the fence, and trotted toward Rifka's house. They heard the crashing and banging, the muffled shouts and screams still coming from the center of town. A woman dragging a little girl ran out in front of them.

"Where are you going?" Leibel asked, skidding to a stop.

"I don't know," she wailed, "Where can I go? I'm alone."

"Go to the bakery—that way," he pointed, and ran on with Rifka.

Suddenly, the noise from the marketplace stopped. They stopped, too, and listened. Dov and the others must have reached the peasants, must be talking to them, explaining, persuading. For long minutes, silence hung over the waiting town. Then a roar of voices rose; then the crash of falling glass. Sharp pistol shots punctuated the roar. Leibel and Rifka grabbed hands tightly.

"The talking didn't work." Rifka whispered.

They ran on to Rifka's house, choking back tears.

In the dark, shuttered kitchen, Aunt Miriam was crying. "I went to Fanya. I begged her just to take Berelleh and Meyer for overnight. Nobody would know they weren't hers. But she wouldn't do it. She was afraid. 'Make a cross on your door,' she said, 'then they won't bother you.' Where can I hide them? What should I do?"

"Be quiet," Mama snapped. "Elli and Berelleh are little enough to fit in the loft above the shed. We'll hide them together. Elli, you're in charge. I'm giving you a bag of candy to help keep Berelleh quiet. Don't budge until I come to get you."

"It's good I got Samson out of here in time," Elli said shakily. Mama gave him a quick hug and pushed him gently out to the shed.

"Rifkalleh, thank heaven you're here," she said. "Run to Reb Leib's house with Aunt Miriam and the baby. He has room for you in the attic. He promised me."

"No," Rifka said, "I don't want to leave you."

"You must," she said urgently. "A young girl like you is in great danger. I have to stay here with Papa."

"Chaykeh, no. I want you to go also," Papa said.

She shook her head.

They all jumped when there was sudden banging at the locked door. Papa peered through a crack in the shutter and then opened the door for red-faced Shloimeh the carpenter, carrying a thick stick, with a hammer tucked in his belt.

"Mosheh," he cried, "come, bring your axe. They're coming down this way. We have to fight them off."

Papa shook his head. "I can't."

"But they're murderers," Chayim cried.

"I can't," Papa repeated softly. "My blood is not redder than theirs. I can't spill anybody's blood."

"But they'll kill us."

"That will be on their conscience—not mine."

The carpenter slammed the door and ran on.

Papa placed the candle on the floor, sat down beside it with his Prayer Book, and holding his prayer shawl as a tent to keep the light from showing at the window he began to recite the afternoon prayers.

"Go!" Mama yelled. Aunt Miriam pressed her youngest to her bulging belly and waddled toward Reb Leib's house followed by Rifka and Leibel.

At the end of the street a door flew open and things began flying out the doorway—pillows, shoes, a clock. A voice was crying, "No, no—stop! Help! Police!" And other voices were

loudly singing the Russian army song that Rifka had heard
on the wagon that same day, a million years ago.

Reb Leib's door opened to Aunt Miriam's desperate
pounding and she was pulled in. Rifka took Leibel's hand
and tugged him down the steps and away.

"What did you do? Your mother said..."

"I'm not going to huddle up there like a chicken in a
coop," Rifka said. They ran on.

Staggering down the street toward them, his red nose
shining, was big Peter, followed by two wobbling friends.
"Happy constootion, happy Lil Father," he babbled, raising
an arm in greeting. A silver candlestick dropped out of his
open shirt.

"Peter, that's Aunt Miriam's!" Rifka cried.

"Oho, Jews!" His friends yelled and lurched toward Rifka
and Leibel. They raced away.

A small man puffed past them. Peter barred his way. "Give
me your money, give me everything you have!"

"No, not me, friend, comrade. I work for the government.
I love the Czar!"

The peasants bellowed with laughter and began to push
Berl the clock fixer between them as he yelled, "Leave me be,
I'm Fedka's friend, I collect information for the government,
I'm on *your* side!"

Leibel and Rifka exchanged shocked glances—Berl was a
traitor—and ran on.

Nobody stopped them.

Through the marketplace, littered with broken glass, bits
of clothing, and pieces of wooden shutters, they ran.
Red-cheeked farm women in gay print skirts and tow-headed
children were climbing around in the broken stores pushing

odds and ends into their sacks — a can of tea, a bit of to-
bacco, a boot. They ran through clouds of snowy feathers in
the streets beyond, where the looters were gaily ripping up
quilts and pillows, past singing, shouting people, past others
lying quiet and bloody across their doorsteps or trembling in
their hiding places.

Once a drunken peasant charged at Rifka with arms out-
stretched, but Leibel kicked ferociously and they ran on as
the man fell.

Suddenly it was all behind them. They were out of the
town and stumbling through the forest undergrowth. They
collapsed into the bushes. In a few minutes, the forest
accepted them. The frogs resumed their evening croaking,
the bedding-down birds finished whistling "good night," the
reeds whispered and rustled. But the muted cries from the
town went on and on — a strange, unnatural mix of crying,
wailing, laughing, screaming.

Wheels rattled on the bridge going toward town. Voices
rose in excitement. "There's so much, you should see — quilts,
white bread, fur coats. My father said to bring the cart, we'd
need it to get everything home..." The sound of voices and
wheels moved away.

"They're not stopping," Leibel whispered. "They'll wipe
out the whole town." They felt helpless and miserable.

A great white shape hovered above and then settled into
the reeds in front of them. A stork was bedding down for the
night.

"A stork!" Rifka gasped, "Leibel, I think I know how we can
get the peasants to go home!"

"How?"

"Like storks. When we were kids we'd sing, 'stork, stork fly away, your house is on fire, your children will burn.' " Rifka whispered. "You and I can set fire to the peasants' huts. The straw roofs will burn quickly and they'll all run home."

"Fire? Where would we get fire?"

Triumphantly, she pulled two of her father's thick matches out of her pocket.

"It might work. We have to try *something*." Leibel's voice cracked with excitement.

"But, but..." Rifka had second thoughts. "Is it a right thing to do? Papa wouldn't agree. He'd say that our wise men tell, 'what is hateful to you, do not do to your fellowmen.' "

"The pogromchiks should've thought of that. Our wise men also said, 'if I'm not myself, who will be for me.' "

Rifka suddenly began giggling, "Leibel," she spluttered, "we're both lunatics. We're arguing about what our wise men said while the whole town is being torn to pieces behind us."

"Let's not argue. Let's go. And call me Ari!"

They ran across the empty bridge. The sky had deepened to blue and the first stars were blinking. In the field, they hurriedly picked dry corn stalks and twisted them together to make torches. They ran on, hearts pounding, through the dark tunnel of woods and out again into the starlit night.

At the first house, the furious barking of the dog met them before they had even started up the path. He was chained to a tree beside the house and he reared up snarling and snapping.

Leibel waited until he was almost within reach of the greedy white teeth, then he lit the torch and thrust it toward the dog. While he held the animal off, Rifka searched the strange house. No people, only three chickens. "Kish, kish, kish," she shooed them out. Leibel lit a second torch and ran around the house setting fire to the shaggy roof-thatch.

They didn't wait to see the flames lick their way up the slope; they were on their way to the next house.

They ducked in the low doorway and found a small boy and girl asleep on straw mattresses. Carefully and quietly, they lifted the little ones and carried them to a cart that was tipped on the path near the road. The children didn't wake up, just as Berelleh and Meyer never woke up when they fell asleep at Rifka's house and were carried home. Rifka ached with guilt as she covered them. We're burning their house, she thought; it's almost winter—where will they live? And then she remembered the frightened eyes of Elli and Berelleh an hour earlier when Uncle Ephraim had carried them up to the loft and covered them with straw. Tears blinded her.

"Hurry," she whispered to Leibel, choking back tears. They shooed the goats and chickens far out into the field and set fire to the second roof.

They ran on and then paused to look back. The first house was a blazing torch against the dying sunset in the sky over Savran. Flames were beginning to nibble at the roof of the second house.

The last house was empty. The entire family must have been in town. "We'll fix them, we'll teach them," Leibel muttered, running around the outside with his torch held to the crackling straw and his red hair glinting in the light of the fire. They hurried to the shed, drove a fat sow out to the field, and hauled out two coops of geese before they set the house ablaze.

All at once, they were both exhausted. They stumbled back

to the road, hand in hand, clutching their torches and the one remaining match.

"Leibel — Ari — I can't do anymore," Rifka apologized, struggling to push her legs forward.

He put his arm around her waist, holding her up, as they walked toward Savran. They heard the terrible sounds again. Faint yelling, small popping noises, and then something new — the far off grinding of wagon wheels on the packed earth and the galloping of a hard-driven horse.

Leibel sucked in his breath. "Get off the road," he cried, "I think we did it!" Skinny, gawky Leibel was suddenly as strong as the Biblical Samson, pulling Rifka on and on and then helping her to hide in the high corn stalks.

The houses blazed and crackled behind them. Wagon sounds grew louder. Soon a wagon rolled past, carrying a frantically shouting load of passengers. A few minutes later, there were more anxious hurrying voices on the road from town.

By the time Rifka and Leibel dragged themselves to the river's edge to hide in the reeds, the sounds of the pogrom had ended in Savran. Feet drummed over the bridge above them for a while. Some peasants were going home carrying their stolen goods, some were going to help put out the fire, but the excited, greedy, hunting sound was gone from their voices. The pogrom was over.

"We did it, we did it!" Leibel kept murmuring, half wondering and half proud. "Just a kid, he called me. Ha! What'll Dov say now?"

Rifka tingled from the top of her tangled, scraggly hair to the tips of her aching toes. "We did it!" she echoed. "We helped save the town."

They were warm against each other. "Ari," Rifka said softly,"Ari is a lion and you were really like a lion, you know."

He grinned, embarrassed. "Lions don't have much imagination," he said. "I'm lucky you were here. I'd never think of such a crazy idea myself."

"I'll miss you when you go to the Land of Israel."

"I'll miss you, too."

Mist settled slowly on the river. They stood up and stretched their stiff legs and arms. It was time to go home and face whatever they might find.

TWENTY

Rifka's Ticket to the World

"Suddenly — a fire, lighting up the whole sky, coming from
no place — like magic. It scared the wits out of the peasants.
They thought God was punishing them. That's what saved
Savran. Take my word for it." Fishkeh waved his herring em-
phatically, splattering Hirsh with brine.

"No, no. Shloimeh and Dov and those others with their
guns and sticks made a big difference. Nothing works like a
strong fist," Hirsh insisted.

The two men leaned against their wagons in the hushed
marketplace the next morning. Other townspeople crept
about sweeping up glass and taking stock of what was left.

"What difference?" Fishkeh scoffed. "Ten men with three
guns and twenty bullets against all the peasants of the
countryside. It was the fires that ended it, I tell you. The
pogromchiks did enough damage. Two people killed, may
they rest in peace, and others with bullet wounds."

"Don't forget about Ephraim's Miriam," Hirsh said,
shaking his head, "Tch, tch, tch."

"You're right, Miriam had a miscarriage and lost her
baby—but that might have happened even if she wasn't
fighting with big Peter. Imagine—a pregnant woman runs
screaming out into the street to get back her candlesticks
from a drunken pogromchik. Unbelievable."

179

Berelleh followed Rifka around all day. He was lost. His mother wasn't yelling at him, slapping and hugging as she always did. She hardly looked at him. She just did her work quietly with her eyes down.

"I can't stand the silence," Ephraim complained to Papa in the bathouse on Friday afternoon. "She's not the same Miriam. I tell her, 'it's not the end of the world, we'll have more children', but she looks through me. She doesn't answer."

"Give her time," Papa said.

Shloimeh the carpenter and his sons, Baruch and Benyah, were loaded with work. Immediately after the pogrom, they had two coffins to make: one for Hanan the tailor's apprentice, Dov's best friend, dead from a bullet in the chest, and another, smaller one for Reb Mendl's youngest child who had been pelted with too many stones by peasant boys as he ran to get home. Elli and his classmates walked to the cemetery beside the small pine box, too bewildered to cry.

The mourners had hardly sat down for the seven days of mourning when the sawing and hammering began again. There was no end to the number of shattered doors, shutters, and pieces of furniture that needed repairing. Baruch had one arm in a sling, Benyah was limping, and Shloimeh nursed two black eyes and a huge lump on his bald head, so the work went slowly.

"Between the three of you — you'll make one sound carpenter," Shloimeh's wife scolded, and whispered a fervent thank you to heaven that she still had them, damaged or not.

Berl the clock fixer had left Savran and gone to another town, where he wouldn't be known as a government spy.

Other people talked of leaving Russia.

"I've been thinking about America," Fishkeh confided in Papa. "I have a cousin in America. He makes a good living selling herring."

"To sell herring, you don't have to go to America."

"No, but to walk down the street with my chin up like a man, I have to go to America."

One day, Rifka went with Shayndel and Raizelleh to visit Dov. He had a bullet wound in one shoulder from the pogrom.

"I brought you such good books," Shayndel said, dumping a pile on his bed. "Economics, politics, history…"

"Not for me," Dov said. "Peter and Sasha taught me more than all those books. As soon as this shoulder heals, I'm off to Palestine. If I get shot there, at least my blood will fertilize my own land."

Raizelleh shivered and made a face.

"You're deserting us, too," Shayndel murmured, and her eyes filled with tears.

Velvl's letter arrived three weeks after the pogrom. When Papa opened it, a slip of paper fluttered out. It was a check for fifty American dollars. Papa read the letter aloud:

Dear Mama and Papa,

I hope this letter finds you well. I read in the newspaper about the pogrom in Odessa after the giving of the constitution. I hope there was no trouble in Savran and Belta. I'm worried about all of you, and about Fraydeh and Yosselleh.

Please, I beg you to come to America. I already sent Fraydeh a ticket and I enclose money for a steamship

       Rifka Grows Up

*ticket for Rifka. Please listen to me. Let Rifka come now
to help Fraydeh.*

*Tell Rifka that in New York, in America, there is a
college that takes in the best students without money,
and they can become doctors or teachers or anything.
The world is open for her here.*

*With Uncle Pinyeh's help, I have already begun to
make weekly payments on tickets for the rest of you. We
can make a good life for our family here. America wants
us as much as we need her.*

Your loving, anxious son
Velvl

"Our whole world is Savran," Mama said softly. "What will
we do in America?"

"God is in America, too," Papa said.

The whole world is open. The whole world. The thought
overwhelmed Rifka. She had to tell Leibel...Ari.

"Mama, I'll be right back."

"Take your shawl; it's chilly. They won't let you into
America if you're sick."

Halfway down the street, Rifka could hear the baker and
Leibel yelling at each other as they kneaded dough for the
next batch of baking.

"No!"

"Yes!"

"No, I won't! You can't make me."

"You're a child, Leibel. I can make you do whatever I
think is right, do you hear me! *Dov*, I can't make—but *you*, I
can make."

Rifka hesitated. She wanted to talk to Leibel, but how
could she break into a family fight?

"Come to Palestine, too," Leibel's voice pleaded. "You can be a baker there."

"To feed the Turks and the jackals? Idiot! There's nothing there. In America, they need bakers. You'll come with Mama and me to America."

"No!"

"Yes! Even if I have to tie you up in a flour sack and carry you — I'll...."

The door flew open and Leibel stormed out, with a trail of flour puffing from his shoes and apron. "No, no, no..." he kept shouting over his shoulder — and bumped right into Rifka.

"Poor Leibel." She patted his hand.

"I keep yelling and yelling," he said sadly, "but my father is right. If he goes to America now, I'll have to go, too. I have no money. I'm too young to get to Palestine by myself."

"I'm sorry," Rifka said sympathetically. "Would it help, would it make any difference to you, that I'm going to America, too? Velvl just sent us the passage money."

His eyes widened, his flour-coated eyelashes blinked, and then he lifted her in a great, powdery, squeezing hug.

"Leibel — Ari!" she cried out and wrestled loose to take a breath.

"It'll help," he said, and his ears glowed red through the flour. "It'll really help. But as soon as I'm old enough, I'm leaving America and going to the Land of Israel. Someday, when you're Madame Professor Rifka Zelikovich, maybe you'll come, too."

Rifka skipped home. Ari would be in America, too, at least for a while. She was so happy.

As she turned into her street, she heard a familiar, operatic voice shrieking, "Berelleh, if I catch you making mudpies again with my Sabbath flour, I'll smack you until you can't sit for a week, and Meyer, you better finish every crumb of your potato or you'll get a spanking, too. You're nothing but skin and bones..."

Sticking her fingers in her ears, Rifka bounded up the steps two at a time. Savran and Aunt Miriam were almost back to normal—as normal as they could be, living on a volcano.